A Thread of Evidence
A Mibs Monahan Mystery

Joan L. Kelly

Full Quiver Publishing,
Pakenham Ontario

This book is a work of fiction.
Characters and incidents are products of the author's
imagination.

A Thread of Evidence
Copyright 2021 Joan L. Kelly

Published by
Full Quiver Publishing
PO Box 244
Pakenham, Ontario K0A 2X0
www.fullquiverpublishing.com

ISBN Number: 978-1-987970-24-1
Printed and bound in the USA
Cover design: James Hrkach
Cover photo: T.M.O. Buildings / Alamy Stock Photo
Cover model: Evelina Zhu

NATIONAL LIBRARY OF CANADA
CATALOGUING IN PUBLICATION

Published by FQ Publishing
A Division of Innate Productions

This book is dedicated to all my brothers and sisters. I have so many memories of us growing up together. It's a wonderful thing to be part of a big family.

Prologue

The wind slapped him in the face as he turned the corner and rushed down the dingy, trash-strewn alley. Clutching the blue duffel bag close to his chest, the scruffy-looking man shivered, not so much from the frosty morning breeze as from the shrill of sirens that pierced the air. When he heard the screech of brakes followed by the slamming of car doors, he knew that only moments separated him from capture and arrest.

He pushed up a cracked, stained lid covering a garbage bin and hesitated. The smell was overwhelming; the putrid trash piled high. If only there were a better place....

Self-preservation took over. "I have no choice."

He hastily put the duffel in and let the lid slam back in place as he continued his escape down the cluttered alley.

~~

Marian pushed open the large cardboard box that had served as her bedroom for the night. She stared cautiously up and down the alley before scooting into the overcast morning. It was early, but not too early, to head over to St. Martin's soup kitchen and line up for a free meal.

Though muddled from sleep, a garbage bin slamming shut caught her attention. People often threw away usable items or even decent food. *Is there time to check?*

Shoving open the heavy lid, she peered into the shadowy interior. Among the torn garbage bags, papers, and other rubbish was a new navy-blue duffel bag. The woman slowly reached a hand down and grabbed the zipper tab. As she began to unzip the top, the pack moved slightly. The movement startled her, and she jumped back. The lid slammed shut with a bang. Her heart pounding, she stared at the lid and sucked in a breath. Pushing the cover all the way up and using a dented bucket to keep it propped open, the street maiden leaned forward and watched the duffel without touching it. A small, mewing sound emanated from the bag. Her stomach sinking, she shook her head. What kind of person would dump an innocent kitten in a trash bin?

If she rescued the animal, she would have to feed it. It was hard enough finding food for herself! Why take on the care of a cat? Her heart battling her mind, she knew that she couldn't let the poor thing starve. The sound from the duffel became louder. Not allowing herself to think about it anymore, she reached down and quickly unzipped the bag.

Marian gasped, slapping her hand against her mouth to hold back heaves of shock as small, scared eyes stared back at her. Tears slowly slid down her face as she gently reached into the bag and lifted the little one out. It wasn't a kitten; it was much more precious.

The baby whimpered louder. Marian held the pink-clothed child close and rocked back and forth. The little one stopped crying, worked a small thumb into its mouth, and began sucking loudly.

"You're hungry, aren't you?" she said. "Don't worry. Mommy will take care of you. Mommy will take care of her little girl."

So began Marian Carpenter's journey home to Havendale, the same day Clara Richmond was found. It was the day Clara Richmond became someone else's child.

~~

While a bag lady across town comforted a three-month-old baby clothed in a pink romper and matching booties, another lady wearing an emerald, green designer dress cradled her daughter, Camilla, in her arms and cried. Her expression reflected both joy and grief. She and her husband, Jackson, had one of their twins safely home, but the other was still missing. Her little Clara was still out there somewhere. No one could tell them if the baby was hot or cold, hungry or tired. No one knew if she was even alive.

Raphael Wayne, a tall, barrel-chested senior FBI agent, leaned down and spoke to Mrs. Richmond. "We've brought one of your daughters safely home. We'll do our best to find the other one, too."

"Can you promise me that?" Crystal Richmond met his gaze straight on. "Can you? You assured us that you had everything covered. You told us that if we listened to you that our girls should be home with us by now and the kidnappers in custody."

Straightening to his full six-foot height, Agent Wayne regarded Mrs. Richmond and then her husband.

What had happened? They had plenty of people at the drop site. They even had police officers stationed on top of nearby buildings. The kidnapper, since identified from fingerprints as one Vince Boston, had passed through the park gate and down to the water fountain where the exchange was to take place. Halfway there, Boston had stopped and noticed the man picking up trash near the walkway. How had Boston realized that it was a trap?

Wayne replayed the scene in his head. The kidnapper had eyed the agent, who was dressed as an employee of the park maintenance department. Shouting a profanity, Boston turned back toward the entrance. As soon as the kidnapper began to run, the undercover agent dropped the trash bag and pulled out a gun as he ran after him. A plain-clothed officer, Jake Wilson, had been behind a concession stand, pretending to set up for the day. Not bothering to take off the apron he wore, he sprinted after the kidnapper and outran the FBI agents. He had almost caught up with the kidnapper when Boston suddenly stopped, turned, and glared at the officer.

"You shoot at me, and you'll hit the kid," he said. "She's in the bag."

Wilson skidded to a stop. He anxiously kept an eye on the backpack Boston slid off his back and held in front of his body. The officer was a good shot but couldn't risk hitting the child. He slowly lowered his gun and motioned for the agents behind him to stay back. For a few seconds, everyone froze in place.

"Set the pack down and step back." Officer Wilson kept his voice calm. "It will go easier on you if the children aren't hurt. You know that." Wilson paused for a few seconds to give the kidnapper a chance to think. "Don't do something that you will regret."

The man gave a mocking reply. "The only thing I'll regret is not getting away from here."

Boston eyed the anxious police and FBI agents waiting for his next move.

Boston screamed, "I'm not going to let you arrest me for kidnapping!" Pulling a gun from his jacket pocket and pointing it at the pack, he demanded, "Put your guns down!"

Agent Wayne paused. Everything depended on

clear direction. "Put your guns on the ground! Everyone! Do it now!"

Jake Wilson slowly lowered his gun to the ground and just as slowly stood back up to face the criminal in front of him. The other agents within sight of the kidnapper did the same. Silence slowly filled the park. Background noise from the surrounding streets faded as all eyes watched Vince Boston.

Boston held the backpack at arm's length and glared at Wilson. "Her or me! You choose."

He threw the backpack high into the air.

Wilson sprinted forward and then dove the last few feet.

Boston began to run toward the park entrance.

"Stop and drop your gun." An officer in police blue had stepped from behind a tree and pointed his handgun at the fleeing kidnapper.

Boston turned and fired at the policeman. The shot sent the officer's hat flying as it creased the left side of his head just above the ear. The policeman staggered but did not go down. He re-aimed at Wilson but did not need to fire. As soon as the kidnapper had fired, a sharpshooter from a nearby building took him down.

As the police handled the kidnapper, Jake Wilson caught the pack and rolled onto his back, trying to protect the bundle he had snatched from the air.

Wilson sat up, unzipped the backpack, and carefully lifted a blanket-wrapped bundle from the bag. Unwinding the blanket, the officer found the baby. She lay so still in his arms that he feared that they were too late. Laying his ear against the tiny chest, he gave a sigh of relief.

"She's still breathing!" he shouted. "Where are the paramedics?"

"They're coming across the lawn now," someone answered.

Another agent, Marcy, pulled a bottle from the backpack. Turning to the paramedics as they reached them, she directed, "Check this bottle. I bet he drugged the baby to keep her asleep."

While attention was focused on the child, Agent Wayne walked over and scrutinized the dead kidnapper.

"We needed him alive!" Agent Wayne snapped. "He didn't bring both girls, and we don't know where he left the other one."

"Sir!" someone yelled. "There's another guy. One of our men on the roof across the street just reported that they saw another man running from the park. He's carrying a duffel bag."

"Stop him! Which way is he heading?"

"He's heading north, maybe to the subway."

"Is he still visible from the rooftop?"

After listening to his earpiece for a moment, the agent shook his head. "Negative. They lost sight of him."

"He may have been watching from somewhere in the park and took off when he saw what was going down with the other kidnapper. Alert every police car in the area and tell them to watch for a man carrying a duffel bag."

Twice they had caught sight of the man who could possibly have the second Richmond baby. Both times they lost him.

~~

Two hours later, Senior Agent Wayne stood in the family room of the Richmonds' exquisitely decorated home, situated in the middle of an exclusive neighborhood.

"What are we going to do now?" Jackson

Richmond's voice cracked as he asked. "How will we get Clara back?"

Sitting down, Wayne rested his elbows on his knees and steepled his fingers together.

"We have officers and FBI agents all over the city searching. We are convinced that Boston was not working alone. The other person or persons may try to contact you again. We need to be ready in case they do."

"What if they don't?" Jackson paused. "What will they do with Clara? Can you tell me, Agent Wayne?"

"I can't know what they are going to do. I hope the kidnappers will contact you, or possibly, if they are scared off, they will leave her someplace safe. Maybe she will be left at a hospital or a church."

~~

The FBI agents soon knew a lot about Boston: where he lived, where he worked and used to work. He had once worked in the park maintenance department. Wayne grimaced. Boston had known something was wrong during the exchange because he had worked for the park. He knew that the maintenance didn't start until 8:00 a.m. He probably also noticed that there were many more people in the park than there usually would be at six in the morning.

Agent Wayne shook his head at the errors in their surveillance. Hindsight didn't help them find the other missing three-month-old. They checked everyone and every place connected to Vince Boston. They checked every call and every tip that was received. But nothing led them to the other kidnapped child.

A month later, they were still searching, but hope was fading.

Chapter 1
Twenty-Two Years Later

Mibs Monahan hurried down the hallway toward her college dorm room. Her thoughts returned to the troubling phone call she had received earlier that morning. Oblivious to those around her, Mibs did not hear the man following behind her. She was surprised when a hand grabbed her arm, pulling her to a stop. The young woman turned to see dark, piercing eyes glaring down at her. Wavy, black hair, straight white teeth, and a dimpled chin gave the man a movie-star appearance. When Mibs had first met him, she considered his smile and his six-foot-two athletic build appealing. Now, she wished that she had never met him, had never gone out on that first date with him.

"Nate, let go of my arm!" Her face tightened.

"Not until you talk to me," he snapped, his hand squeezing her arm as he jutted his chin forward.

"We don't have anything to talk about. I've told you a dozen times to leave me alone."

"You know that you don't mean that. You can't just walk away from me, Mibs." His eyes glistened. "I love you. We belong together."

She winced as Nate's grip tightened. "You're hurting me! Let go!"

Mibs heard a swishing sound followed by a thump as a large burgundy purse connected to the side of Nate Olsen's head.

He released his grip and grabbed his head.

"She said to let go, you jerk!" an angry voice demanded.

Mibs rubbed her arm as she watched the tall, ebony-skinned woman now positioned between her and Nate.

"The girl does....not....want....to....see....YOU!!" Red-tipped black curls bounced as she shook her head and jabbed her finger at the surprised man. "Get out, and don't let me see you bothering my friend again."

Anger swept across Nate's face before he huffed and turned away.

Mibs watched his shoulders hunch and his hands clench into fists as he moved down the hall.

A shiver shook her slim body as she realized how scared she felt. "Thank you, Whitney. He really took me by surprise." Mibs touched her friend's hand. "I thought that he'd finally stopped bothering me."

Whitney folded her arms across her ample chest, her lips compressed, a disapproving arch to her brow, and shook her head. "I told you, ya need to file a restraining order on that guy."

Mibs raised her hands in frustration. "I just don't understand him. We only went out a few times. I never even gave him a quick kiss goodnight. The next thing I knew, he was insisting that I see only him. Texts and calls every day! I'm sure I saw him following me several times, too. I don't want someone who's possessive." She took in a deep breath and slowly exhaled. "He really upsets me!"

Whitney engulfed Mibs in her gold silk-clad arms. "Friend, he's what they call a stalker. You should report him."

"Well," Mibs sighed as she stepped away and

considered the taller woman. "We're graduating, and we'll go our separate ways. After this week, he should be out of my life."

"I hope you're right," Whitney emphasized.

"I can't worry about him right now. I have to hurry," Mibs said, waving off the concern. "I have to get home right away."

"What do you mean by right away?" Whitney's blouse and matching slacks made a soft swishing sound, and the scent of her jasmine perfume wafted around them as they continued down the hall toward the room they shared. "I thought you were starting your internship at that design company next week and wouldn't head back to Havendale until the Fourth of July."

"I had to change my plans," Mibs sighed.

Closing the door, Whitney questioned her friend. "Okay, so what's going on?" She tilted her head and stared at Mibs. "What is it?"

"It's Aunt Bernie. She fell and was rushed to the hospital." Mibs sat down slowly on the powder blue comforter covering her bed. "She broke her hip, and surgery is scheduled for tomorrow morning."

Whitney sat down next to her. "Oh no. I'm sorry. I know she's like a momma to you. Do they think she'll be all right?"

Mibs forced back the tears as she thought about her Aunt Bernie, the only mother she had ever known. "The doctor said that it was pretty serious because of her age and her osteoporosis." She leaned over and grabbed a Kleenex from the box on her nightstand. "I forget about Aunt Bernie's age. For so many years, I never thought of her as being a lot older than my classmates' parents. It wasn't until I started high school that I noticed changes.

Going up and down the stairs, carrying groceries, and other little things she had done all her life were getting harder for her. She started taking naps during the day and going to bed earlier." Wiping her eyes, she tried to smile. "She was already in her sixties when I was born. Aunt Bernie has taken care of me all these years. Now it's time for me to take care of her."

"But wouldn't getting a good-paying job be the best way to do that?" Whitney asked.

Shaking her head, Mibs answered, "She's going to need round-the-clock care after her surgery. The doctor said she'd probably be in a wheelchair for a while, and she'll need to go to physical therapy."

They sat quietly for a moment. "You could hire a nurse. That way, you could do the internship and work on your master's degree like you had planned," Whitney offered.

"No, I won't do that," Mibs stated, "not after all she has done for me. I need to be the one to take care of her. I have to be there for her," she insisted, wringing her hands in worry. "I won't let a stranger take care of her when I'm perfectly capable of doing it." Mibs' voice faltered for a moment. "What if she takes a turn for the worse?"

Mibs stood, walked to the closet, opened the door, and pulled out a suitcase. "I was able to get a ticket for the train that leaves at 5:30 this evening, but I'm hoping you could do a couple favors for me." She tossed items into the bag.

"Sure, whatever you need," Whitney agreed without a second's hesitation.

"Since I won't be back for the graduation ceremony, will you return my gown when you take yours back?"

"You're not even going to walk up for your diploma?" Whitney moaned, shoulders slumping. They had been planning the day for the last month, what they would wear, where they were going to celebrate. It was supposed to be their last hurrah before becoming *real* adults.

"I don't think I'll be back at all," Mibs whispered. "This brings me to the other favor, and it's a big one."

Whitney nodded. "Well, lay it on me! What else do you need?"

Waving her hand around the room, Mibs smiled at their bulletin board with pictures, playbills, announcements, and notes, the scarves Whitney had lovingly twisted around the two flea-market lamps and various souvenirs of their senior year. "What would it take for me to convince you to pack up all my stuff? I don't even care how it's packed just so it's ready to move by the end of next week. Tom and Peter, the two guys from my calculus study group, live in the same part of the state as I do. I told them that I would pay for the gas if they brought my stuff and dropped it off on their way home. But, now, I won't have time to get it boxed up."

Whitney nodded. "Promise to call me and let me know how your auntie is doing," her friend insisted, "and how you're doing." Her eyes traveled around their shared space. "I'm sad you're leaving, but we'll always be friends."

Mibs nodded and hugged her friend. "I promise."

The tall, dark beauty glanced in the mirror at herself and at the shorter, fair-complexioned roommate. Whitney joked, "We look enough alike

13

to be sisters, don't ya think?"

Mibs laughed through her tears. "You need glasses." She added, "But you'll always be a sister in my heart."

Chapter 2

Bernice Monahan leaned against the car window and smiled when she saw the cream-colored, two-story house come into view. After a week in the hospital and another two in the rehab facility, she was more than ready to be home. Having been healthy most of her life, getting old aggravated her. Nevertheless, with the help of God, she was going to meet this challenge the same way she had faced others: straight on and full-steam ahead.

The car pulled into the driveway and stopped close to the front steps. A sizeable flowering quince had been growing by the west side of the house for years; it was gone now. In its place, newly stained, a wooden ramp was attached to the porch.

Mibs opened the car door with a flourish.

Bernice pointed to the ramp. "When did that happen?" she asked. It matched the original porch, and if she didn't know it was new, it wouldn't have stood out.

"I hired a contractor to put it in ten days ago," Mibs said, swallowing hard. "The doctor said that you better get used to this wheelchair; you're going to be in it for a while." Patting Bernice's wrinkled hand, Mibs teased, "If you wanted someone who could muscle you and your chair up a set of porch steps, you should have adopted a big, husky nephew instead of a needle-and-thread-toting niece."

Reaching to caress Mibs' cheek, Bernice replied, "I'm more than happy with what I got."

~~

After getting Aunt Bernie settled on the sofa with a crocheted blanket around her legs, Mibs put a cup of tea on a small table within her reach. She sat down in the chair across from her aunt.

"Are you comfortable, Aunt Bernie?" She picked up the cozy-covered pot and poured tea for herself in a delicate Blue Willow teacup.

Her aunt's soft white hair shimmered as she slowly nodded. "Yes, I'm fine." Picking up her teacup, she took a small sip and studied her niece. "Mibs, I can always tell when you have something on your mind." The cup rattled lightly when she placed it back on the saucer. "Are you wishing that you hadn't turned down that internship? I can get someone to stay with me. You shouldn't give up your life for some old lady."

"Don't talk that way!" Mibs' brows furrowed in irritation. "You're not just 'some old lady', and no, I'm not thinking about the internship."

"Then what is it? There's something you want to talk about," Aunt Bernie said.

Sighing and nodding, Mibs said, "You're right, as usual. I do have something important to ask you. I've been busy while you were recuperating, thinking about how I can work and still take care of you. After praying several Rosaries and asking the Holy Spirit for guidance, I came up with a solution. I hope you'll go along with my plan."

Mibs got up from the chair and went over to the sofa. Sitting on the floor near her aunt and resting her arms on the cushion, she studied her beloved great-aunt. The old woman's pure white hair had thinned over the years, and soft curls formed a halo as the lamplight shone through them. Despite her age and the trauma she had been

16

through in the last few weeks, there was still strength and brightness shining in her hazel eyes.

Mibs took a deep breath and asked, "Aunt Bernie, would you be willing to sell this house?"

"Sell this house?" Rubbing her hand across her forehead, Aunt Bernie turned away for a moment. When she made eye contact with Mibs, she was smiling in relief. "Mirabelle, I've wanted to move into a more efficient house for a long time, but I thought it would be too hard on you. You've done without so many things all your life; I didn't want to suggest that you give up your home."

~~

Bernice thought about how she had struggled with keeping the budget balanced over the years. After her brother, Henry, and her niece, Marian, both died, there was no one left to care for little Mirabelle except Bernice. When she adopted Mibs, Bernice's savings supplemented her social security. The house was paid for, and her brother had put it in her name. They made do, but it wasn't always easy. Because Mibs had earned an excellent scholarship, the money Aunt Bernie had squirreled away over the years had been almost enough to pay the remaining tuition, room, and meals. Mibs worked two jobs while carrying an A average in her classes at the university. Her heart swelled with pride for her dear girl.

"Really?" Mibs gaped, surprised. "You should have said something!"

"Well, I'm saying it now. What did you have in mind?" Bernie asked.

"Give me just a minute," Mibs responded, jumping up.

Mibs ran up the stairs to her room. She was

17

back a few moments later with a folder. Opening the folder and setting it on her aunt's lap, she explained. "I've already talked to a realtor. This lists the values of similar houses in the area and information about the realty company." Mibs hesitated. "Actually, the paperwork is ready. All it needs is your signature. Oh, Aunt Bernie, I hope you aren't upset with me for taking over like this, but I thought that it would be for the best."

Bernice chuckled and then placed her hand on her niece's arm. "I guess I taught you well. I've never hesitated when things needed to be done, and I'm happy to see that you are willing to take charge when needed."

"I'm glad you said that," Mibs declared, "because there's more to my plan."

"Oh? What else do you have in mind?" Bernice asked.

"What I have in mind is a place to work and live all wrapped up in a nice package. Well, in this case, it isn't a package; it's a building," Mibs bubbled with excitement.

Bernice tilted her head to see better. "I guess you better explain."

"I found a store at the west end of Main Street that has a small apartment above it." Hesitating for just a moment, Mibs said, "I want to reopen Monahan's Sewing Shop! A business like you had before you retired."

"A sewing shop." Bernice blinked.

Mibs rattled on. "Please, hear me out, Aunt Bernie. You've admitted yourself that I'm one of the best seamstresses that you've ever seen." Smiling, she winked at her aunt and added, "Of course, that's because *you* taught me."

Shaking her head and smiling back, Bernice

said, "Go on. Tell me more."

"With my fashion design and business degrees and with all the knowledge you gained and all the connections you kept from your seamstress shop days, I know we could do it." Taking a quick breath, Mibs continued, "I'd be doing something I love; we'd have a place to live, and I'd be there to help you!"

The two Monahan ladies eyed each other for a few minutes, one with a sprinkling of freckles across her young face and the other with soft-brown age spots dotting her features. Each studied the other, hopefully optimistic.

"Well, what do you think, Aunt Bernie?" Mibs broke the silence. "I know your fingers don't hold a needle well anymore, but your mind is still sharp. I could do the seamstress work and bookkeeping. You could take care of the counter and phone when you feel up to it. You could help with the ordering if you prefer or help keep an eye on the inventory. Do as much or as little as you want."

~~

"Hold on, girl. Give me a minute to digest all this," Aunt Bernie said. There was a spark in the old woman's eyes that hadn't been there for some time. Picking up the cup and saucer from the small table, she took the time to finish her tea before she answered. "Let's do it!"

Mibs hugged her aunt. "Let me show you what I have in mind. We'll need to do some renovating. The last business that occupied the building was a consignment shop, and the one before that was a used bookstore. Besides the main room, there are two good-sized rooms in the back. We'll make one of them into a bedroom for you, so you don't have to worry about any steps. The other can be organized into an office and storage area."

"My lands! You sure have been busy." Aunt Bernie beamed. "Well, let's see your notebook so you can fill me in on the details. Then, you better call that realtor and have him bring those papers over so we can get this adventure started."

Chapter 3

Six months later, while Aunt Bernie was arranging items on the counter in Monahan's Sewing Shop and Mibs was in the back room organizing inventory, Mibs heard a customer's bubbly voice. A mop of dark hair showed just above the multi-colored bundle of clothing that moved through the entrance. A round, plump face peeked around the clothes and smiled.

"Hello, where do you want these costumes?" the woman asked.

"I'll get it," Mibs told Aunt Bernie as she came to the front of the store.

After the woman deposited the colorful outfits on a central table, she turned toward the seamstress. "Hello, I'm Mrs. Anita Barns from the Community Theater. Are you Miss Monahan? You appear awfully young." The woman pursed her lips. "Are you sure that you can handle all these? We must have everything ready by the end of the month."

When Mrs. Barns finally stopped to catch her breath, Mibs interjected. "Don't worry, Mrs. Barns. Everything will be done in plenty of time. Do you have specific repairs, or do you just want me to inspect each one and check their condition?" Mibs picked up a costume, mentally noting the frayed lace and missing rhinestones.

"Some of the outfits do have a paper attached listing things like tears or missing buttons, but we would like you to check them to see if anything else is needed," the woman said.

After pulling a sketch pad from a nearby shelf,

Mibs held it out to the woman, opening it slowly. "Here are the sketches that I drew up for the other costumes you described on the phone. Would you like to see them?"

Mrs. Barns greedily accepted the pad. She devoured the drawings, lingering over some and turning back to others. Her bright, red-tinted lips turned up in a smile. "Why...these are lovely, simply lovely." Tapping the top sketch with pumpkin-colored nails, she exclaimed, "The committee will love this!"

"I'm glad you like them." Mibs exhaled with relief. She had spent a lot of time working on these designs. "I'll bring them by for the meeting Thursday night."

"If these costumes turn out as nice as the pictures, I'm sure you'll get a contract as the dressmaker for all our plays," Mrs. Barns giggled with delight. "We've had some of these outfits for a long time. They are getting worn and need to be replaced. Everyone in the theater group would be thrilled to have a talented seamstress available." Inspecting the shop, she noticed a dressing screen in the far corner of the store. "Is that room divider for trying on outfits? You do fittings, don't you?"

Mibs nodded. "Of course. I can do them here or, possibly, at the theater. We can discuss that when we finalize any details."

Grabbing Mibs' hand, Anita Barns pumped her arm up and down enthusiastically. "Wonderful! I'll see you in a few days!" The bells on the door chimed a goodbye as the energetic woman hurried out of the store.

After she left, Mibs turned to her aunt. "Did you hear that, Aunt Bernie? We may get a long-term contract."

"Of course, you will, Mibs. You're good at what you do." The older woman wheeled her chair from behind the counter. "With the homecoming dresses that you finished, we're doing pretty well for only being open three months."

Mibs nodded. "Yes, we're off to a good start." Setting the sketch pad back on the shelf, she pointed to a clothing rack in the corner. "I better tackle that mending, too. I enjoy creating and sewing costumes and party dresses, but I still have to get the regular mending and alterations done promptly."

"Yes, you're right about that," Aunt Bernie agreed. "Why don't I help you finish the inventory? Then you can get started on the sewing."

"Sounds good to me," she said.

It was almost closing time when Mibs hung a long-sleeved dress shirt on the clothing rack and wrote out the receipt to go with it. She turned to Aunt Bernie, who was counting down the cash drawer. "Replacing the buttons on this shirt was the last item on my mending list – well, except for the costumes for the Community Theater. If I can get them mended tomorrow, I can take them with me to the meeting."

"That would be nice. I'm sure the theater club would be surprised to get them back so quickly."

The sound of the bells drew their attention to the front door. Two middle-aged women hesitantly entered. Mibs' educated eye noticed that both ladies wore good quality, well-fitted clothing. Expensive but tasteful attire, her aunt would call it. One of the women used a cane and moved slowly into the store. The second woman carried a large, lidded basket on her arm.

"Good afternoon, ladies. May I help you?" Mibs asked.

"I certainly hope so." The clear voice from the first woman belied her frail appearance. "I have some dear friends who need help."

"Oh?" Mibs tilted her head, confused. "Who are these friends, and how can we help?"

A combination of a snort and a laugh came from the woman holding the basket. "My sister, Jasmine, has always called our dolls 'friends'." Setting the basket on the counter, she opened the lid and lifted out a china doll with a dress made of layers of royal blue taffeta.

"How beautiful!" Aunt Bernie exclaimed. "She must be quite old."

Jasmine reached up to touch the doll's matching blue bonnet. "Yes, she's over 100 years old."

The hands that gently caressed the china head were curled and stiff. They didn't match the young-looking eyes and the face that hinted that the woman could not be over forty-five.

Aunt Bernie wheeled her chair from behind the counter. "Mibs, get some chairs for these lovely ladies. If we sit at the table, it will be easier for them to show us their dolls." As she positioned herself at the end of the wooden table, she introduced herself. "I'm Bernice Monahan, and this is my niece, Mirabelle. I believe your sister called you Jasmine."

"Yes. I'm Jasmine Hornsby," she replied. "And this is Jennifer Morris."

Jennifer placed a steadying hand on Jasmine's back as her sister sat down on one of the chairs that Mibs had brought to the table.

"Could I get anyone something to drink?" Mibs asked.

"No, thank you," Jennifer answered. "We're fine."

As soon as the two women were seated, Aunt Bernie nodded at Jasmine Hornsby and very bluntly stated, "My problem is osteoporosis and arthritis. I'm guessing yours might be some type of severe arthritis."

At first, Mibs thought that her aunt's comment would offend Ms. Hornsby, but instead of getting upset, Jasmine smiled. "I see from your wheelchair that we share a lack of mobility." Nodding, she explained, "I've had rheumatoid arthritis for many years. Most people don't realize that it can strike at a fairly young age."

"Life can be hard sometimes," Aunt Bernie said. "But it's nice to meet a person who faces her problems and keeps going."

"Aunt Bernie," Mibs interrupted. "I think that the ladies came to talk about repairs for their dolls."

"Oh, we don't mind. Do we, Jennifer?" she asked, glancing at her sister. "We have to put up with people all day long who tell us what they think we want to hear. It's refreshing to talk to someone who says what she thinks."

"That's true, Jasmine," Jennifer answered. Turning to Mibs, she said, "Perhaps, a bit of tea would be good. That is, if we aren't taking up too much of your time. I realized that it is almost five. That's when you close, isn't it?"

"We usually do close at five, but we sometimes make exceptions," Mibs said.

By the time the sisters were on their second cup of tea, despite the age differences, the four ladies were chatting like old friends. It was explained that both sisters had enjoyed finding and collecting exquisite and often rare dolls, but it was Jasmine who had always done the sewing. Now, her illness had crippled her hands so severely that she could no longer make the delicate stitches required for their 'friends.'

"I've tried sewing, but I've never had the talent that my sister had," Jennifer explained. Pointing to the large display window that faced Main Street, she added, "Those outfits in the window are quite nice. In fact, that peach-colored dress is just like one I saw in a dress shop when I was in New York a few months ago. It was your window display that drew us here."

"Mirabelle is a wonderful seamstress, and she keeps up with the latest fashions," Aunt Bernie proudly proclaimed. "You'll see a new outfit displayed in the window almost every month."

A loud tap on the glass-windowed entrance door interrupted the ladies. Mibs quickly got up and went to see who it was.

"Hi," a young man wearing a moss-green jacket with a Bicker's Florist logo on the front greeted her. "The sign says that you close at five, but I saw people through the window. I hope it's okay to make this delivery."

"Oh, of course," Mibs said as she accepted the long, slender box that he held out. "Just one moment, please." She hurried over to the counter and returned with a tip for the delivery boy.

~~

Setting the white cardboard box down at the end of the table, Mibs opened it to reveal three beautiful, long-stemmed, red roses.

"How lovely," Jennifer said.

"Who are they from?" Bernice asked.

Mibs lifted a small envelope from the box and

26

pulled out the card. Her smile faded, and the color had drained from her face.

"Is something wrong?" Her aunt frowned. "Who are they from?"

The girl quickly stuffed the card into the pocket of her smock and closed the box. "J...just an o...old acquaintance."

Bernice's eyes narrowed as she observed her niece but did not question her. Instead, she turned to the Hornsby sisters. "You said that you had other dolls that needed care."

"Yes, we certainly do," Jasmine affirmed. "We've been collecting since we were young girls. Mibs, do you make house calls? Some of the members of our collection are incredibly old and delicate, and we hate to take them out of the house."

Jennifer leaned forward and whispered confidentially, "We have no problem paying whatever extra you may charge. Our grandfather came from what used to be called *old money*, and he invested well. We are quite able to pay for quality work."

"I would love to inspect your doll collection and give you an estimate on any work that may be needed. As far as the quality of my work, I try to do my absolute best for each of my customers, no matter who they are."

Jasmine replied, "Good."

"We'd better get home," Jennifer suggested to her sister. "I don't want to listen to James complain if he has to wait for dinner."

"Oh, I forgot to tell you that James won't be home until late tonight. He has to work over again." Jasmine sighed. Addressing Bernice and Mibs, she explained, "James is my husband. Perhaps he will be at the house when you come to see the rest of our doll collection."

"Do you have any children?" Mibs asked.

"No, unfortunately not," she responded. "I married late in life, and perhaps with the way that rheumatoid arthritis has affected me, it is better that way." With another sigh, the woman grabbed hold of the tabletop and started to pull herself up.

Jennifer quickly rose to help her sister. A frown creased the woman's face as she mumbled, "Yes, it's probably better, considering how often James has to work late."

~~

Mibs wasn't sure if anyone else had heard the comment. Apparently, Jennifer was not happy with her brother-in-law.

After the ladies gave instructions on how to get to their country home, Mibs followed them to the door and locked up for the day. When she turned around, Aunt Bernie was staring up at her.

"Now, young lady, who are the flowers from, and why did that card upset you?" she questioned.

"I can't hide anything from you, can I?"

"Not when I can tell something is bothering you."

The girl's shoulders drooped, and she returned to the table and opened the flower box. She ran her eyes over the beautiful roses for a moment before shutting the top again. She marched to the back room and dumped the package and card into a large garbage bin before returning to her aunt. Kneeling in front of her, she answered, "They're from a guy named Nate Olsen. I went out with him a few times in college."

Aunt Bernie waited quietly for her to continue.

"It didn't take long for me to realize that he was not someone with whom I wanted to get serious.

The problem was that he had other ideas. He wouldn't leave me alone. He kept coming by my dorm room until my roommate, Whitney, threatened to call the police. I thought it was over until flowers and presents started showing up a few weeks before graduation. I should've reported him, but I figured that when we both left college, I would never hear from him again." She sat back on her heels and shook her head. "He knew my hometown was Havendale, but he didn't have my address or phone number. He may have seen the paper with our advertisement about the store opening, or he could have easily found information on the internet. It isn't that hard to find a person with today's technology."

Aunt Bernie brushed her age-spotted hand across Mibs' hair. "Your friend, Whitney, was right. Promise me that if he sends anything else, calls – anything – you're going to report him."

"Okay. I promise." Mibs stood and kissed the old woman's soft, wrinkled cheek.

Chapter 4

"Good morning, Mr. Hornsby," the girl said. Scrutinizing eyes peered up over the top of a pair of reading glasses. "Mr. Conway has been waiting for you. He expected you ten minutes ago." The secretary's voice sounded judgmental as she reached over and pushed a button on her desk phone. "James Hornsby is here."

"Send him in," a voice replied.

"Thank you, Helen," James Hornsby said. He hesitated in front of the desk. "Helen, I haven't asked you lately about how things are going with you. Has your daughter had her baby yet? Is everyone doing fine?"

The secretary gazed at the accountant standing in front of her before she answered, "My grandson was born two months ago. Everyone is doing fine. Thank you for asking."

"That's good. Glad to hear it." James shifted his feet as if he were going to say more.

At that moment, the office door opened, and one of the receptionists from the front lobby came in carrying a gold-colored, rectangular box. "This was just delivered at the front desk. It's addressed to Mr. Conway."

"Thank you, Cindy." Helen took the box from the receptionist and read the card attached to the top. "It's from that salesman Mr. Conway talked to yesterday."

"Since I'm going into his office, would you like me to take it to him?" Hornsby offered.

"If you don't mind." The secretary handed it to him.

James spent the next twenty minutes discussing

pending accounts with his boss. They were just finishing up with the last one when Mr. Conway's intercom buzzed.

"Yes, Helen, what is it?"

"You're due at a staff meeting in ten minutes. You said that I should remind you."

"Thank you, Helen. I'll be right out."

When Mr. Conway stood up, James began gathering his papers and slid them into a tan briefcase. He nodded at the gold box. "It must be nice to get gifts. Does that happen very often?"

Conway shrugged. "Not too often, usually just when someone is trying to make an impression." Picking up the gold box, he noted the lettering across the top. "*Chocolate Covered Peanuts*. Well, these would be wasted on me because I'm allergic to peanuts."

"Really?" James said. "They're my sister-in-law's favorite. My wife likes the soft-centered kind, but her sister goes for candy with a crunch."

Handing the box of chocolate to James, Conway offered, "Why don't you take them? They'll just go to waste sitting here."

"Why...thank you, sir. I'll do that."

Later that night, James Hornsby pulled into the three-car garage attached to a stately brick and stone mansion. He turned off his BMW and pulled the box of candy from where it had slid under the front seat. He puttered around in the garage, and several minutes passed before he made his way into the house. Entering through the kitchen door, he almost ran into Janie, their live-in cook and housekeeper.

"Oh, Mr. James, excuse me. I was just leaving. I told some friends that I would go to the movies with them."

"Have a good time, Janie," he said, motioning for her to leave. "Oh, by the way, is there any of that fudge that you made the other day left?"

"Are you hungry, sir? I can stay and fix you a dish." Janie began to take her jacket off.

"No, no, don't stay. I was just going to take some in with this box of chocolate peanuts. My boss gave it to me, and I know that Jennifer would like them, but I think Jasmine would prefer the fudge."

"Well, isn't that nice? The fudge is in that red-colored container on the counter," the housekeeper said, pointing.

"Go and meet your friends, Janie. I'll get it."

Chapter 5

Mibs studied the ornate numbers attached to a square brick column: *928 Willow Road.* A wrought-iron gate stood open and revealed a hedge-bordered driveway.

"This must be it," she muttered to herself. Lifting her foot from the brake pedal of her ten-year-old Ford sedan, she headed down the drive. As Mibs maneuvered around a curve at the end of the hedge, she slowed down. A beautiful two-story brick and stone house came into view. Stunning flower beds edged the well-maintained yard that led to a wrap-around porch. An elegant home was what she expected. What she didn't expect were the ambulance and police cars parked in front. A truck was parked near the manicured lawn, and people streamed in and out of the house.

Unsure of what to do, Mibs stopped without the usual squeak of brakes, glad that she'd had the car serviced yesterday, and watched with foreboding, chills racing down her arms. She had met the two friendly and interesting women four days ago. Had something happened to the sisters? She bowed her head and said a silent prayer for the Hornsby household.

A knock on the car window startled her.

Rolling the window down, she was addressed in a firm tone by a tall, brunette woman wearing a police uniform. The officer smelled of peppermint and wore a name tag with *M. Schroeder* across it. "Ma'am, do you have a reason for being here?"

Nodding, the girl replied, "I have an

appointment with Jasmine Hornsby and her sister, Jennifer Morris. Officer, what's wrong?"

Instead of answering, the policewoman offered a dismissive head shake. "What's your name, ma'am?"

"My name is Mibs...ah, Mirabelle Monahan. I'm a seamstress and was asked to come by today and discuss some sewing work," she answered with trepidation.

Pointing to a spot next to the truck, an ocean blue Chevy Silverado, the officer directed, "Park your car over there and turn it off. Stay in the vehicle until you receive further directions." When Mibs pulled up close to the truck, she noticed that it was a newer style, its bed filled with plywood and cans of paint.

She had just shut the engine off when she saw two men wearing EMS jackets bringing a stretcher out the front door. Mibs' heart dropped as she realized someone had died. The men had reached the wide walkway when Jasmine Hornsby came through the doorway. She tried to follow the medical personnel but had to grab a large plant stand near the entrance to keep from falling. She was unsteady without her cane, and Mibs could see the pain on her face as tears streamed from her eyes.

"Jennifer," she cried, reaching out toward the stretcher.

Forgetting the officer's instructions, Mibs jumped out of the car and ran to Jasmine. "Mrs. Hornsby." Mibs put her arm around the frail woman. Embracing Jasmine's limp body, Mibs felt stunned by how light she was. The woman was skin and bones. "Let me help you. I don't want you to fall."

The grief-stricken woman turned to her. Recognition filled her eyes. "Mibs," she whispered, sadness and devastation lining her face. "Jennifer...Jennifer; she's gone."

"Please, come in and sit down, Mrs. Hornsby. I think you need to get off your feet," a deep, concerned voice directed them.

Mibs turned to see a well-dressed, broad-shouldered man standing near the doorway. Her artist's attention to detail took in the fact that he was about eight inches taller than her five-foot, seven-inch height. His chestnut-colored hair appeared to be naturally curly, but she could not decide on the color of his eyes. They seemed to have shades of blue, flecked with specks of gold. His single-breasted suit had a notched lapel, and a burgundy-and-cream-striped tie went well with the soft brown color of his jacket and slacks.

The man stepped closer and took Jasmine's other arm. "Why don't we get you inside? The housekeeper is making some tea." The words were a question, but Mibs could hear the authority.

Both turned toward the door to head back into the house. Mibs' heart unexpectedly jumped when his tanned hand brushed against hers as they guided Jasmine into the home.

As soon as the distraught woman was sitting down in a ribbon back chair at a table in a small alcove, the man turned to Mibs, his blue eyes flashing with appreciation. "Thank you for your help, Miss...."

"Mibs Monahan," Mibs replied.

~~

The man folded his arms across his chest for a few seconds while he continued to study the young woman in front of him. She seemed young, but there was a quality there in her bright green eyes. Wisdom and hard-learned lessons peered back at him, at odds with her physical appearance. Shaking his head, he focused again on the reason he was there. What he needed to do was investigate this death, not wonder how the reddish-gold locks would look hanging loosely around her soft face.

"Miss Monahan, what brings you out here today?" he asked brusquely, forcing his mind back into investigative mode.

The girl took time to respond. "I'm here to...it doesn't matter now. I need to comfort my friend." She considered him for a moment. "And who are you? Why are you here? What happened? Did Jennifer have a heart attack?"

His jaw tightened with every question she asked. Slowly he reached into his jacket and pulled out a slim wallet. Opening it, he showed her his identification. "Detective Sergeant Jace Trueblood, Miss Monahan. The EMS personnel notified the police when they determined that Miss Morris' death wasn't from natural causes."

~~

"What!" Mibs exclaimed. "What does that mean?"

Jasmine began sobbing so hard that her shoulders shook.

Mibs turned and sat down in the chair next to the middle-aged woman, putting her arms around her. "I'm so sorry, so deeply sorry. I know that I just met you and your sister, but Aunt Bernie and I felt like we were friends by the time you left our shop. Is there anything I can do? Anything at all?"

Mibs glanced at Janie, the housekeeper: ash-blond hair, slightly plump figure but with a tall, erect posture and compassionate eyes surrounded by light brown lashes. Sadness etched the housekeeper's face. "I got a hold of the doctor," Janie said. "He called in a prescription for a sedative. I think that it would be best if you lie down and rest for a while."

Janie had set an ornate, silver tea service down on the table.

"No. I can't rest until I find out what happened to my sister," Jasmine insisted.

After pouring a cup of tea and then stirring in a large spoonful of sugar, Janie set it in front of Mrs. Hornsby. "Drink a few sips of this. It may help."

Mibs stood up and touched the detective's sleeve, directing him away from the table.

"Detective Trueblood, what did you mean when you said it wasn't a natural death?"

He gave her an impatient smile. "Natural death means dying in your sleep, suffering a heart attack, having a stroke. You know, natural?"

Mibs bit back the angry retort on the tip of her tongue. What had she been told? Would she get more flies with honey than vinegar? Detective Trueblood appeared to be the kind of man used to the bitter taste of life; his suspicious eyes and tense body language screamed 'stay away.' She would have to ask Aunt Bernie, but as far as she knew, there weren't any Truebloods in Havendale.

"Besides, I'm the one who needs to be asking the questions." He glowered at Mibs. "Why don't you tell me why you showed up here this morning?"

Mibs nodded. "Jennifer and Jasmine asked me to come by today. I'm a seamstress, and I repaired some of their antique dolls. I had an appointment to come by and examine the rest of their collection.

I was going to do some more sewing work for them. Apparently, they have taken good care of the dolls over the years."

~~

"I see." Jace Trueblood rubbed his chin as he considered what she had said. Dolls. Were women in their late forties still playing with dolls? It wasn't the strangest thing he'd heard after over ten years on the Nashville police force, but it was odd. Maybe it would help. "I'm not sure if it would be better for you to leave or if having you proceed with your original plan of looking at this doll collection would help distract and calm Mrs. Hornsby."

"I would be glad to do whichever is better for Jasmine." She nervously rubbed her hands together.

"Okay," he slowly nodded. "Why don't you sound Mrs. Hornsby out and see what she would like to do? I need to be able to talk to her today. Maybe you and this doll discussion will calm her down."

~~

Mibs ignored the derision in his voice as he flipped through his notebook. She studied the serious face in front of her. "Detective, what do the emergency technicians think happened to Jennifer?"

Taking a deep breath, Jace shook his head. "You're not going to go all Jessica Fletcher on me, are you? This isn't TV, Miss Monahan."

"Yes, I know that, Detective."

He guided her farther away from the alcove and the still-distraught Jasmine Hornsby.

He smelled like soap and spice, the warm scent teasing her senses as he leaned down and lowered his voice.

"As soon as they started checking Miss Morris, they noticed indications that she had been poisoned."

"Poisoned," Mibs whispered, eyes widening in surprise. *Who would want to hurt that sweet woman?*

Detective Trueblood's face was blank, like he had been so disillusioned by humanity that nothing could surprise him anymore. "Apparently, Miss Morris is normally an early riser. This morning, she wasn't out on the patio with her second cup of coffee as usual when the housekeeper came down to make breakfast. Mr. Hornsby left for work early today, so he was already gone. Miss Morris still hadn't come down by eight-thirty." Nodding toward Janie, he continued. "The housekeeper went up to check on her, found her on the bathroom floor, and called an ambulance. By the time the ambulance got here, she was dead. Besides the signs of vomiting and seizures, they noticed her enlarged pupils and her skin's blue color. These are all signs of severe poisoning."

"Was it accidental?" Mibs nibbled on her lower lip.

"We have to determine that. No one else seems to have been affected, so we're trying to narrow down what Miss Morris was exposed to and what she ate. If it is an item that another person can encounter, we need to find out." Leading Mibs back to the small table, he directed her to see if she could help calm the grieving sister. "The sooner that I can talk to her, the sooner we may be able to pin down what killed Miss Morris. Waiting for the toxicology report may take too long if there is a toxic item around, and others may have been exposed."

A short time later, the sedative for Mrs. Hornsby was delivered. She took only one tablet instead of two, as the doctor recommended. However, the half-dose, along with Janie's and Mibs' comfort, seemed to calm her down. Mibs suggested that Jasmine show her which dolls had been Jennifer's favorites and try to focus on the good things in her sister's life.

"I think that I would like that. I'll show you Jen's very favorite; she was a cloth doll named Cassie." Jasmine's expression seemed to drift into memories.

While Janie helped her employer to the chair lift attached to the stairs, Mibs ran to her car to retrieve the basket of dolls that she was returning. As she came back into the house, Detective Trueblood was waiting for her. He was standing out of the way of the forensic team but close enough to keep an eye on things.

"Mrs. Hornsby seems to be pulling herself together." He nodded with appreciation.

"Yes," Mibs agreed, thankful she could help. "If you can give us another twenty minutes or so, I think she may be able to talk to you."

The left side of his mouth quirked up slightly. "That'll work; it'll give me time to interview the housekeeper."

~~

Jasmine sat on the edge of a sea-green love seat as Mibs reached for the indicated doll. "That's Cassie. Jennifer has had her since she was eight years old. Cassie is made completely out of muslin, and her hair is cream-colored embroidery thread. It took over a thousand stitches to make the intricate flower design on the dress."

"She's beautiful." Mibs carefully ran her hand along the material. "She has such a simple elegance about her." Mibs noticed a variety of embroidery stitches. Besides the basic straight stitch and the stem stitch, she saw delicate lazy-daisy stitches and hundreds of French knots. "This handwork is unbelievable. How did Jennifer keep it in such good condition for so many years, especially from only eight years old?"

"That can be credited to our mother. Mom knew how much work our Aunt Cecilia – she's the one who made it – had put into the doll. She insisted that Jen did not go outside with Cassie and that Jen put her up anytime we were eating or drinking. After a while, it became second nature to make sure Cassie stayed clean and stain-free." Tears formed in Jasmine's eyes.

"Oh, I'm sorry," Mibs apologized. "I wanted this to comfort you, not make you cry."

Jasmine wiped her eyes. "It is comforting. These are good memories, but I don't think anything can keep me from being upset right now." She pointed. "Please, set Cassie there on the dresser so I can reach her later and hand me that little one with the red dress."

Ten minutes later, the same policewoman who had directed Mibs to pull her car over when she first arrived knocked on the door. "Excuse me, Mrs. Hornsby, but Detective Trueblood would like to talk to you now, if you feel up to it."

"Yes, I'll be right down." Jasmine turned to Mibs. "I know Jennifer was impressed by you and wanted you to take care of our doll friends. Would you come back in a week or two and go through the collection with me?"

"Of course, I will. And if there is anything else I

can do in the meantime, just give me a call."

Mibs helped Jasmine to the chair lift and then followed her to the bottom of the stairs. As Mrs. Hornsby stood and leaned against her cane, Janie brought in a wheelchair.

"I know that you don't like to use your wheelchair unless you are exhausted," Janie addressed Jasmine, "but I think it would be a good idea right now."

"Okay, maybe you are right." The frail woman sank into the seat.

Just then, James Hornsby rushed through the front door. Seeing his wife, he ran to her and knelt in front of her chair.

"Dear, are you all right? I can't believe what the police told me on the phone. Is Jennifer really...is she really dead?"

Biting her lip to keep from crying again, Mrs. Hornsby nodded. Her husband rose and put his arm around her for a moment before pushing her chair to the living room.

Mibs saw Officer Schroeder standing near the door. Approaching, the seamstress tapped her shoulder. "Would it be all right if I go home now?"

"Let me check with Sergeant Trueblood and see if he's okay with that," the officer responded.

Mibs followed slowly behind while she walked toward the detective who had just sat down across from the Hornsbys. She could hear him say that the housekeeper could think of only two things that Miss Morris had eaten or come in contact with, which no one else had touched: the new azalea bushes that she was working with in the garden and the chocolate-covered peanuts that she ate last night.

~~

"Some plants such as the azalea are toxic, but I can't see Miss Morris eating any of the plants. Also, there are gloves that she apparently wears while working in the garden." Jace Trueblood clasped his hands and rested his elbows on his knees as he leaned forward and watched the couple sitting on the sofa. Jace studied Mr. and Mrs. Hornsby for a moment. If Jennifer Morris had been married, the first person he would suspect would be her husband. Next would be the children. Anyone angry with the woman would be checked out too. Except, from what he'd gathered in the past two hours, Jennifer was a sweet woman who'd never married and had no children. His first case in Havendale and the suspect pool did not seem promising.

"What about the candy? Did either of you eat any of it?"

James Hornsby stood up and scratched his forehead. "The chocolate-covered peanuts," he moaned.

"Did either of you eat them?" Jace asked, concerned. If they had, he'd need to get their stomachs pumped right away. Just what he needed—a double or triple homicide on his hands.

"No, no, I didn't eat any, but I'm the one who brought home the box of candy. Please, tell me that they weren't what poisoned her." James flailed his hands in the air, giving the detective a beseeching gesture.

"We don't know what the cause was yet. I've already sent the box to the lab to be checked. Is there anything else that either of you can think of that Jennifer had that no one else did?"

"Excuse me, sir," Officer Schroeder cut in. "Is it all right if Miss Monahan leaves now?"

43

Shaking off a flicker of impatience at the interruption, Jace reminded himself that in a small town like Havendale, things were a little more casual than in the large, populated city he had come from. Studying the young woman standing behind Schroeder, Jace slowly nodded. Miss Monahan had been more help than he'd honestly expected. His gut was telling him she was a trustworthy person. "I don't see any reason for her to stay. Just make sure you have her phone number and address."

"Yes, sir," Schroeder responded.

~~

Mibs gave the requested information and then walked to her car. She wished that she could help Jasmine. The only thing she could think of was to pray God would shower the grieving sister with the extra grace and guidance that she would need over the coming days. Mibs would pray for Jennifer when she attended Sunday Mass.

Chapter 6

Five days after her visit to the Hornsby House, Mibs worked at the sewing shop while Aunt Bernie was at a nearby diner having a long lunch with one of her friends. Mibs was unpacking a new shipment of material and had just examined a bolt of colorful fleece prints when the door opened, and Detective Jace Trueblood sauntered in.

The afternoon sunlight beamed through the open door, outlining his broad shoulders and highlighting the reddish-brown tones of his chestnut hair.

Setting the thick fabric down on her worktable, she watched him cross the room, reproving herself for the feeling of butterflies that suddenly hit her stomach. Why would his appearance cause her to feel this way when only a few days ago, she considered him unapproachable?

Today he was dressed more casually. The forest green tie he was wearing had been pulled slightly loose, and the first button of his dress shirt was undone. His thick hair looked like he had run his hand through it several times, leaving tufts of curls standing on end. That, along with the missing scowl he had worn the other day, gave him a more youthful appearance.

"Detective Trueblood," she greeted him, her throat growing dryer with each step he took. "What can I do for you? Is there anything new on the case we need to talk about?"

"I just left the Hornsby house." He shook his

head; a smile tugged at the corner of his lips. He had warned her about trying to play detective. Unconcerned, Mibs shrugged.

"As you can imagine, Mrs. Hornsby is still quite upset about her sister's death." He ran his hands over a bolt of beautiful linen fabric, the turquoise material looking fragile in his rough, calloused hands. "We have the report back about the poison. I'm telling you that there isn't anything toxic in the house since you're planning on going back to the Hornsby home."

"Thank you for letting me know. Does that mean you know what killed Jennifer?"

"Lindane." Jace gave her a searching look, which she returned, causing him to rub the back of his neck. "It's used as an insecticide."

"Was it on the plants or bushes that she had been working with in her garden?" Mibs pondered the possibility. She'd never heard of the insecticide, but she didn't have much of a green thumb, either.

"It's already been leaked to the press, so I guess it won't hurt to tell you," Jace said, drolly throwing a searching glance her way. "It was in the candy, the chocolate-covered peanuts."

"Oh, my!" Mibs exclaimed. After a moment's thought, she whispered, "Then, it *was* murder."

"We've switched our investigation over from Mr. Hornsby's house to his office."

"His office? Why?"

"The box of chocolate was sent to his boss, Mr. Conway. He gave it to Hornsby when he realized it contained peanuts, which give him a severe allergic reaction. Miss Morris was likely killed by mistake. The intended victim appears to have been Mr. Conway, vice-president of Bernstein

Electronic Company."

Dropping onto a nearby chair, Mibs shook her head. "How sad. Poor Jennifer. And poor Jasmine. She will miss her sister so much."

~~

Jace took a step forward and extended his arm but stopped before he placed his hand on the woman's shoulder. Fearing a lack of professionalism, he let his hand drop to his side. Still wanting to comfort her, he knelt on one knee, so they were face to face. "Are you all right?"

"Yes, I'm fine. It's just so sad."

Nodding, he cleared his throat. "Well, the main reason I came by was to tell you the house is no longer considered a crime scene. You're free to go and see Mrs. Hornsby. She seems to be a nice lady and apparently likes you. Anyway, I thought she might enjoy it if you came to visit or do whatever doll...ah," Jace paused, eyes darting around as he searched for the right words, "*things* needed to be done."

Jace accepted Mibs' thankful nod, her teeth worrying her lower lip for a moment. Her reddish-gold hair was twisted in a fancy braid, showing off her long neck and shell-like ears. Her green eyes called to him, and Jace found himself staring at her for a second longer than was necessary. Standing up abruptly, he gave Mibs a jerky nod before marching across the shop floor. *What was wrong with him? What was it about this girl that had him so distracted?*

He quickly opened the door, calling over his shoulder, "Have a good day."

~~

Mibs listened as the sound of the bells faded after the door closed.

Smiling sadly, she said out loud, "Well, Detective Jace Trueblood, you may be a tough lawman, but I think you have a bit of a soft spot, too."

Chapter 7

Light rain greeted Mibs as she stepped out of her car at the Hornsby estate precisely four weeks after Jennifer's death. The young seamstress had planned on bringing her aunt along to visit with Jasmine while she worked with the doll collection. However, the sudden dampness set Aunt Bernie's joints aching. With her arthritis making its presence excruciatingly known, it was decided that staying home inside the warm building was a better choice for the aging woman.

Mibs and her aunt had attended the funeral of Jennifer Morris and visited Jasmine to check on her and view the collection. But this was the first time Mibs had returned to the house to continue working on the dolls. She anticipated spending a couple of hours with Jasmine on what she hoped would give the woman a brief respite of happiness.

Balancing an umbrella in her left hand, Mibs used her right to pull a sewing box out of the back seat and then slammed the car door shut. Hurrying up the front steps, she stopped on the roofed porch long enough to give the umbrella a few good shakes. Before she could reach out and push the doorbell, the sound of a car making its way up the long drive caught her attention. Mibs watched as the housekeeper, Janie, pulled a champagne-colored SUV into the parking area.

Janie's hooded raincoat protected her from the drizzle as she scurried to the back of the vehicle and removed two large bags. Mibs met her halfway down the steps and held the umbrella over the bags of groceries. When they were under the porch's protection, Janie set one of the bags down and dug into her pants pocket for the front door key.

"I'm so sorry that I wasn't here to greet you," Janie apologized. "I always do the shopping on Saturday, but I thought that I'd be back half an hour ago. The lines at the market were terrible! Then, it started raining, and I'm just not comfortable driving in the rain." The flustered housekeeper prattled on as she opened the door and ushered Mibs into the vestibule. "Did you ring the doorbell? I left Ms. Jasmine up in the doll room, and it takes her several minutes to come down if I'm not here to answer the door. I told her that I'd be gone for less than an hour. She's probably wondering what's taking me so long."

"I just got here," Mibs calmly assured her. "I was about to ring the bell when you arrived."

"Oh, good. I'm glad you didn't have to wait." Janie set the bag down on a small, round table and slipped out of her raincoat. After hanging it on a carved-wood coat rack that stood just inside the entranceway, she accepted Mibs' coat and umbrella, putting them on the other side of the stand.

Mibs set her sewing box against the wall and stepped back through the door to grab the rest of the groceries from the porch. "Why don't I help you carry these into the kitchen?"

"Oh, thank you." Janie smiled gratefully. "Just follow me."

As the two women passed through the living room, the housekeeper turned toward the stairway and yelled, "Jasmine, I'm back! Miss Monahan is here, too!"

Janie hesitated for just a moment when there

was no reply. "Well, maybe she didn't hear me. Let's get the groceries to the kitchen. Then, you can go on up if you remember where the doll room is."

"Yes, it's the third door right of the stairs, correct?"

After setting the damp grocery bags on the marble-topped kitchen counter, Mibs retraced her steps through the living room and headed up the carpeted staircase. Rapping on the door to the room where Jasmine Hornsby kept her extensive antique doll collection, Mibs waited for an acknowledging voice to welcome her. When there was no answer, she knocked again and then reached for the doorknob. To her surprise, the door was locked.

"Jasmine," she called, "Jasmine, it's Mibs." A knot of tension clenched her stomach.

When there was still no response, she hurried back down the steps and into the kitchen to get Janie.

"I can't get Jasmine to answer me, and the door is locked."

"The door is locked?" Janie exclaimed, shock accentuating her face. "That door is never locked!"

The two ladies quickly returned to the closed door. After confirming that the door was locked and that Mrs. Hornsby was not answering, Janie checked each of the upstairs rooms. Mibs ran back downstairs, searched the first-floor rooms and the outside patio before rejoining the housekeeper at the locked door.

"She isn't anywhere in the house or outside. I don't understand." Janie's forehead wrinkled in concern. "There must be something wrong!"

"I think we'd better open the door," Mibs

prompted. "Where is the key to this room?" She tried to present a calm demeanor, hoping to keep Janie from getting upset.

"Key? There is no key. You could lock it from the inside if you wanted. There is an old slide bar-type lock." The housekeeper shook her head and added, "It was used as a guest room for a while, but that was years ago. I don't remember it being locked by anyone since then."

"We better call for help. Something must be wrong." Mibs pulled out her phone.

~~

Detective Jace Trueblood directed the forensic team to the stairway before turning toward the two ladies waiting anxiously a few feet away.

He wished that he didn't see Mibs Monahan here, under these circumstances. He often went to the same coffee shop she frequented. In the past month, he had run into Mibs enough to know that if he weren't so busy with his new job and a major remodeling project, he'd be spending time with her. There was something about her that he couldn't shake, and yet he knew that between working on his inherited house and the still-unsolved murder of Jennifer Hornsby, he shouldn't be thinking about her at all.

Taking a slow breath, he stepped across the hardwood floor and gestured toward the sofa in the nearby living room. "Why don't we sit down and talk?"

Mibs and Janie headed to the sofa as Detective Trueblood moved a leather-covered ottoman closer, sat down, and leaned forward. "One of the firemen said that you called 911 because you believed Mrs. Hornsby possibly needed help, and you couldn't get into the room. Is this correct?"

"Yes." Janie wrung her hands. "Tell us what happened! All the paramedics and firemen would say was that she was dead. That they needed to call the police." A soft sigh came from her throat as she continued, "I don't understand. She was fine when I left earlier. What happened?"

Resting his elbows on his knees, Jace did not answer her. "Why don't we start from the beginning? Tell me exactly what happened this morning. Start from when you first talked to Mrs. Hornsby and everything that you remember up until the time I got here."

"I don't know," Janie moaned. "I don't know what happened."

"Detective." Mibs shot him a perturbed glare.

He was obviously pushing the poor woman too hard.

"I know you have to ask questions, but it's apparent that Janie is terribly upset. She was more than just a housekeeper and cook for Mrs. Hornsby and Miss Morris. She's been with them for over twenty years and has lost both within a few weeks. Please, can't this wait?"

"I know that this isn't easy, but I need information. Two deaths in the same house within a noticeably short time doesn't happen every day in Havendale. The department is going to want some answers." Forcing a calm tone into his voice, the detective continued. "Why don't we start with what you know, Miss Monahan? When did you arrive? What can you tell me?"

~~

Mibs stared at his strong, handsome face. Although Detective Jace Trueblood was probably only in his early thirties, she had a feeling that he had seen a lot during his time on the police force.

Over coffee, he had told her that he had previously worked as a detective in Nashville before joining the team in Havendale. Mibs wondered what it would be like to get to know someone like this man, who had learned to think things through and find answers. The detective was the total opposite of most of the guys she had met at college, especially Nate Olsen. Pulling her gaze away from the intense, blue eyes, Mibs tried to concentrate.

"Well," she said, "it was a little after one o'clock when I arrived. I was just going to ring the doorbell when Janie pulled up and parked. I helped her carry the groceries into the kitchen. Mrs. Hornsby didn't seem to hear us when we came in, so I went up to the room to greet her. That's when I realized that the door was locked. She didn't respond to my knocking or my voice, so I came down to get Janie. We did a quick search in case she was somewhere else in the house, but we couldn't find her in any of the other rooms or outside. There is no key for the door; I'm not strong enough to break the door open, and so we decided that we needed to call for help."

"And that is when you called 911?"

"Yes, that's correct."

~~

"Now, Miss Monahan, I understand that when the firemen arrived, they found you had leaned a ladder against the window at the back of the house." Jace studied her. It was a rather smart thing to do. She was quick-witted and intelligent; she also seemed to have a calming effect on everyone around her. That is, everyone except him.

Mibs nodded. "Yes, I began thinking that if Jasmine needed immediate help, maybe I could reach her before the fire department could get here from town. I asked Janie if there was another way into the room, and she told me that there was only a window. I ran around back and glanced up, trying to figure out a way into the room. I found a ladder in the garage and was going to try reaching the window with it. That's when the fire department showed up."

In between jotting down notes into a small, thick notebook, Jace carefully watched her eyes and facial expressions. She was expressive but reserved. It wasn't easy to get a quick read on her. When she stopped talking, he encouraged her to continue. She was a dream witness. Clear, direct, and informative. It didn't hurt that her voice was like a soft melody. "Go on. What happened then?"

~~

Mibs tucked a loose strand of hair behind her ear and sat back on the sofa. She wasn't used to having her palms sweat. "Well, when I heard the sirens as the emergency vehicle came up the lane, I propped the ladder against the back wall of the house and hurried around to the front. Two firemen were heading toward the front entrance. I joined them and showed them to the closed door."

Janie picked up the story. "I was still standing in front of the locked room and calling out to Jasmine." Wiping her eyes with a lace-edged handkerchief, she added, "I kept hoping that Jasmine would answer me."

"I noticed that the door was not broken in," the detective said. "I understand that the fireman used a ladder and entered through the window?"

"Yes," Mibs confirmed. "They were going to pry the door open. But when I mentioned the back window and ladder, they decided it would be better to try that way first instead of breaking in the door."

Detective Trueblood nodded. "That corroborates what the firemen told me." Running his hand through his hair, an action which Mibs realized was a habit while he was concentrating, he said, "Okay, what happened then?"

"A fireman had broken a pane of glass in the window, reached through, and opened the lock. We heard the bolt slide. Then he let the others into the room." Mibs paused, thinking about the brief seconds she'd peered into the room. With the emergency personnel blocking the doorway, she couldn't get a clear view.

"But he wouldn't let us in," Janie sobbed. "He let the other fireman in. Then, he motioned for one of the paramedics who had arrived right after them to enter, but he insisted we wait in the hall."

Mibs put her arm around the housekeeper's stout shoulders. "Janie kept asking if Jasmine was all right. Finally, the older of the two firemen stepped out of the room and told us that Jasmine was dead and that we should wait downstairs."

"Please," Janie begged, hysteria rising. "Can I see her? I can't believe she's dead. Not her, too!"

Shaking his head, Jace studied the housekeeper. "No, I don't think it would be good for you to see her." His voice dropped to a more comforting tone. "Apparently, Jasmine Hornsby has committed suicide."

The color from Janie's face drained away. It seemed as if she might faint as she sat there, shaking her head. "No! That's not possible. She would never kill herself. I know she wouldn't do that!"

"Her sister's death hit her pretty hard," Jace

said, his eyes narrowed at her insistence. "Sometimes, pain, whether physical, mental, or emotional, can cause a person to do something they wouldn't normally do. The loss of her sister, combined with her health issues, could have been more of a strain than people around her realized."

"No, I can't believe that," the housekeeper insisted as she buried her face in her hands and wept quietly.

~~

Jace wasn't sure that he believed it either. He found it interesting that this woman couldn't explain what had happened that morning before Mibs had shown up. He figured that she was simply too distraught to think clearly, but he made a quick note to check into the housekeeper and her relationship with the sisters. The detective believed that the housekeeper was just as she seemed. However, he had met some incredibly talented murderers in his law enforcement career.

Mibs glanced toward the stairway as she heard the footsteps and voices of the emergency personnel. She turned away as the covered stretcher was moved out of the Hornsby home.

Janie slowly got up. "I'm going to my room. I need to be alone."

Jace nodded; all he had were suspicions but nothing concrete. In fact, his gut was telling him that the woman's grief was real, and she would never have hurt the two sisters who employed her all these years. But he had to investigate all possibilities.

Mibs reached out and touched Janie's arm. "Before you go, give me the name of someone I can call for you. Do you have family or friends nearby?"

"I have nieces and nephews, but they live out of

57

state. My friends, Sarah and Nan, would come." An expression of overwhelming grief marked the housekeeper's face. "Yes, maybe it would be good if they came over for a while."

~~

After getting the phone numbers for Sarah and Nan, Mibs made sure that Janie was resting before returning to the living room. She would not want to be a detective, not if she had to treat everyone as a suspect. Janie had probably not noticed the hardening of Detective Trueblood's face or the way he watched them. But Mibs had. "If you are through with your questions, I'll call Janie's friends and see if one of them can come over to be with her."

"I do have more questions." The blue in Jace's eyes intensified as they connected and held Mibs' eyes. He turned away and opened his notebook. "But you can call her friends first."

Taking a deep breath, Mibs headed to the phone in the kitchen. She reached Janie's two friends, and they quickly agreed to come over. Mibs' stomach clenched when she returned. She knew where his line of questioning was going. "So what are your questions?" Mibs asked, sitting in the chair opposite him.

"I hope you understand that part of my job is exploring all the angles," he emphasized, a slight frown marring his face before he continued. "It's quite a coincidence that you have shown up right after two different, unnatural deaths."

Mibs' mouth dropped open as his statement soaked in. "Are you accusing me of something, *Detective?*" she snapped.

His lips twitched before he responded. "I'm simply doing my job, *Miss Monahan.*"

Wringing her hands, she inhaled a deep breath and took a moment to control her anger. Trueblood was doing his job. He thought that Janie was a suspect, which was ridiculous. Janie loved the sisters like they were her blood, not her bosses. Now he was questioning her! "I explained why I was here, and I have been trying to cooperate in every way I can."

~~

Jace closed his notebook and stood up. Her eyes were flashing, and if he didn't know better, he would think that Mibs Monahan wanted to throttle him. He had asked around about her. Subtly, of course. He wasn't sure why he was so interested. If it were strictly for his investigation, he wouldn't care who knew, especially when it seemed like she was more interested in bolts of fabric than him.

Everyone said the same thing. A sweet young woman who cared for her aging aunt. Strong-willed. Intelligent. Compassionate. Caring. Generous. No one had described her as cruel or nefarious; he didn't see that in her either. He doubted most people ever saw a hint of irritation, let alone the flare of anger now flashing at him. He liked it, though. She wasn't a pushover, even if she was as sweet as spun sugar, which one of the older guys at the Elks Lodge had said.

"I appreciate that," he offered slowly, wondering at himself. He was investigating another crime in the same home, and all he wanted to do was continue talking to her. She was no more a suspect than his deceased great-uncle who'd left him the two-story Georgian Colonial style monstrosity he was renovating two blocks off Main Street. "Look, I want to believe you, but I don't really know you. It's my job to scrutinize everyone involved. To find answers." As he walked toward the entrance, he looked back, mentally yelling at himself the entire time. "I'm going to speak to the men outside. That's all for now, Miss Monahan, but I'm sure I'll have more questions for y'all later."

~~

Mibs sat there for a few minutes, too stunned to move. "He doesn't really know me?" she muttered, a frown on her face. She had seen him several times during the last few weeks at the little café just off Broad Street. Last week he'd even bought coffee for her. They weren't friends, at least not yet, but she had thought.... *It didn't matter.* She muttered, "He will have more questions later?" He didn't really think she had anything to do with what happened, did he? "He has to study all the angles?" she growled under her breath. Standing up, she clamped her mouth shut. While he was off finding answers, she was wondering about the dolls. Without stopping to think about it, she headed upstairs. Something wasn't right about Jasmine's death.

The firemen and EMS personnel had left. Now, the room was occupied by members of the police crime scene team. The investigators were concentrating on their work, and no one noticed her standing in the doorway. From the doll room entrance, she saw one of the wheelchairs that Mrs. Hornsby occasionally used when her legs were aching more than usual. A photographer was snapping pictures of a pistol that lay by the right side of the chair. A man stood by with a plastic bag in preparation for collecting the weapon.

Mibs' stomach churned when she saw the bloody splatters on the chair and the floor. She leaned against the door frame to steady herself when she saw Cassie, the favorite cloth doll that the two sisters cherished for years. Cassie was leaning against the footrest of the wheelchair. Blood had soaked into the muslin dress, covering much of the delicate stitch work. The young seamstress unconsciously took a few steps into the room as she stared at the doll.

"What are y'all doing here?" Jace rumbled. He stood in the doorway behind her.

Mibs gasped, and she put her hand over her heart.

"I'm sorry if I surprised you, but you shouldn't be in here."

Mibs stared at him for a moment, still smarting from his earlier insinuations. So, instead of apologizing, she declared, "Janie's right."

"What do you mean?" his voice rose in surprise. "Right about what?"

"Mrs. Hornsby didn't kill herself."

"What?" He gave her a searching look. "What makes you say that? Is there something you haven't told me?"

Running her eyes over the chair again for several seconds, Mibs then took in the rest of the room. She had a knack for noticing things out of place. She loved those games where you had to compare two pictures that seemed to be the same, but there were hidden differences. This room was no different. She turned to the detective. "There is no way this was a suicide! First, because she was holding Cassie, and second, an old pistol like that would require a lot of pressure on the trigger to fire; she didn't have that kind of strength in her hands." Pointing to the slide bolt, which had been used to lock the door, she added, "And how could she have reached the lock? Her rheumatoid arthritis was so advanced that it prevented her from raising her arm more than shoulder level."

~~

Jace thought that he had learned to keep his 'poker face' firmly in place. In his line of work, he couldn't afford to let anyone know what he was thinking. He swallowed hard. This was one of the few times that he was bewildered. Jace agreed with her assessments, which was why he was treating this as a homicide. Not that he'd told her that. The idea that Mrs. Hornsby could have reached the bolt on the door or pulled the trigger on the old Colt 45 would have been laughable given her physical atrophy. As part of his investigation into Jennifer Morris's death, he had gotten a medical report on Mrs. Hornsby, something that had seemed over the top to the other guys in the department. But he'd learned a long time ago never to take anything for granted.

"Who the heck is Cassie?" the surprised detective blurted out.

"Cassie is the doll." Mibs pointed to the one in question. "She's stained with blood. Jasmine and Jennifer keep her clean, and ..." She hesitated. "They've ... protected her from damage and stains since they were little. Jasmine would never have been holding that doll if she were going to do something like this."

Jace was trying to make sense of what the woman in front of him was saying. The dolls again! Sure, they may be expensive, but this business about keeping one safe? That didn't make sense to him. However, he wasn't a doll collector. Plus, Mibs seemed to have good instincts about their importance. They had comforted

Jasmine Hornsby before. Would she really be so depressed to kill herself in the one room that brought her joy? Though it wouldn't change the fact that both the door and window were locked from the inside. Someone certainly wanted everyone to believe that Jasmine Hornsby had killed herself. He had a sinking suspicion that it was tied to Jennifer Morris's death.

"Listen, *Nancy Drew.*" His frustration was getting the better of him. "Let the police department do their job and stay out of the way!" If someone were willing to go to these lengths to fool the police, what would they do with the sweet seamstress?

~~

Mibs put her hands on her hips and locked eyes with him. She wasn't a child to be patted on the head and sent on her way. Why would someone kill Jasmine? He should be considering that and not chastising her. "Your investigative team should see if there is another way into this room. I've heard of old houses like this having secret entrances hidden in them. I'm telling you this woman did not shoot herself with that gun!"

He glared at her in return. "And I'm telling you that under certain circumstances, people can do things that they would not or could not normally do!"

~~

Jace realized that he had raised his voice; a few of his colleagues had frozen in mid-motion. They were staring at him and the feisty redhead with amusement. He knew he was a curiosity; he had only been in Havendale three months and on the job for six and a half weeks. His reputation for being an outstanding detective had been whispered in the halls of the police headquarters. There was speculation as to why he moved to Havendale. And here he was going toe to toe with the sweetest woman in town. Why was he letting her get under his skin? He had never allowed anyone to elicit a reaction like this from him. Stepping back, he folded his arms across his chest.

Exhaling a slow breath, Jace shook his head. "Miss Monahan, would you please leave this room and wait downstairs? In fact, why don't you just leave? I don't believe we need anything else from you now, and I have your phone number if we need to contact you."

"Very well, *Detective*," she snapped. "I'll leave, but why don't you find out what really happened to Jasmine Hornsby?"

"Listen!" Jace realized he was raising his voice again and stopped himself. Taking a calming breath, he softened his tone. "I will give this investigation the professional attention that we give all our cases."

~~

Mibs' anger, not so much from what he had said but from the violent loss of two new friends, seemed to drain away. She still thought he was arrogant and not really seeing the same things she did, but it wasn't his fault. Not really. He didn't know the sisters the way she did. Nor could he possibly understand how devoted they were to the dolls. They were much like family, just as much as Janie was. She dropped her gaze. "I'm sorry. I shouldn't have gotten so upset. It's just that I think something happened here that isn't what it seems. I didn't mean to interfere."

"I'm going to walk you to your car, Miss Monahan," he told her crisply.

"No, that's okay. I can see myself out." Mibs turned and stepped to the door. As she did, she looked up at the metal loop that the bolt slid into to lock the door. She stopped when a speck of blue caught her eye. Studying it more closely, she realized it was a piece of thread.

"Detective Trueblood," she called.

"What now, Miss Monahan?" he sighed, walking over to her. "I thought you were leaving."

Mibs scanned his face, realizing that his few wrinkles were a little deeper today, and there was slight darkness under his eyes. He seemed tired. She pointed to the lock. "Did you notice this?"

He leaned in. "Did I notice what?"

"There's a piece of blue thread caught on this part of the lock."

"Thread?" Taking a closer look, he asked, "Why are you pointing out a piece of thread?"

"Well," Mibs hesitated. He obviously needed her help. "What is it doing there? That's a strand of royal-blue silk thread, the same kind I used to repair the dresses on several of the dolls in the collection. I left a spool of it here because I planned to use it again. How would a strand of it get caught in that spot?"

Leaning his head to the side, Jace let out a long sigh. Clearly, he was humoring her. "I don't know how it got there, but why do you think a small piece of thread is important enough to point out?"

Frowning, Mibs tilted her face up and offered a clipped response. "It *could* be evidence!"

"I'll decide what is or isn't evidence, Miss Monahan." Pointing to the doorway, he gave her a stern frown. "It's time for you to go."

After staring at the detective for a few more seconds, Mibs turned and stiffly marched out the door. Infuriating man! He should at least listen to her. He couldn't really be that oblivious to what was going on, could he? Muttering a stream of unflattering opinions, she stormed down the stairs.

~~

Jace waited until he heard the footsteps of the spirited young lady reach the front of the house, the door slamming as she exited before he turned to his investigators. "Benson, any chance you found another way to get out of this room?"

"Sorry, Detective." Todd Benson, a grandfatherly type, well-respected by his peers and a senior crime scene technician, rubbed his chin, perplexed. "We checked for hidden panels and trap doors. Even the window was a no-go. It appears that it had been firmly shut before the firemen forced it open. The only way in or out of this room is the door."

Jace nodded his thanks, disappointed. Addressing the man who was taking pictures around the room, he motioned toward the doorframe. "Samuel, take a close-up of this part of the lock. Take shots from several different angles."

After the photographer was finished, Jace took a small evidence bag out of a case sitting on the floor. Using a pair of tweezers, he carefully removed the piece of blue thread and slipped it into the container.

Chapter 8

A few days later, Detective Jace Trueblood walked into the bullpen. He had a small glass-enclosed office in the back corner of the bustling department. Jace usually left the door open; he missed the comradery of being at one of the scarred and battered desks.

As a sergeant in the detective unit in Nashville, he'd just been one of the guys; here, he was the lead detective, given the title of First Sergeant and the position Chief of Detectives. He had to make time for his work and help the rest of the team improve their skills by working cases with them. It made for some late nights, but the truth was, his life was more relaxed now than ever before. Even with the added job responsibilities and the house, it was a different kind of stress. Not the type that could give him an ulcer or make that third beer seem tempting. During his last check-up, the doctor had indicated that he was developing high blood pressure. That was not a good thing to hear at thirty-one. Inheriting the house on Maple Avenue had given him a reason to move away from Nashville and, hopefully, some of the stress.

Pausing to stare at the newly affixed sign on the glass wall, he shook his head. *Jason Trueblood. Chief of Detectives.* It took him a minute to pry it loose, laughing good-naturedly as the other detectives ribbed him.

"Something wrong with your nameplate, Trueblood?" Sergeant Brice Long teased.

Another detective chuckled. "I hear those big

city detectives can be awful particular about their names."

When Jace had arrived, he'd been certain some of the older guys would resent his new position; they'd been there far longer than he'd even been a cop. Yet, they had welcomed him with open arms. As a detective, he'd solved more cases than the Havendale police department had reported collectively in the last ten years. With so few deaths in this town, the men and women of the detective department wanted a clearance rate better than their current one, which meant everyone in the department, from the evidence clerk to the medical examiner, was on board with him being hired. In return, he focused on helping them by sharing the knowledge he had acquired over the years. Jace turned to toss the nameplate into the trash, only to come up short as the maintenance worker, Walter Kahn, watched him, aghast.

"Is something wrong, Detective?" Walter asked, his waxy white complexion turning beet red. From what he knew about the man, Walter was a retired electrician who hadn't been able to make ends meet on his small pension. He had gotten a job working for the firm that had the city's janitorial contract. The squad had adopted the seventy-something man several years back, and every time the contract was renewed, Walter was one of the few faces that transitioned. Glancing at Juan Mendoza, Jace handed the sign to Walter. Juan and the other guys in the office knew that his legal name was Jace, derived from his two grandfathers' names, *Ja*mes and *Ce*cil. It was a pet peeve of his that people assumed it was short for Jason. He realized that someone had ordered the nameplate.

"My name is Jace," he offered without censure.

"Not Jason?" Walter confirmed, staring at the sign and then glimpsing the other detectives; several of them were smirking.

"No," he agreed, watching recognition and then amusement glitter in Walter's eyes.

"I'll get you a new sign right away, sir." Walter took it and walked away, the sign sliding out of his hands and onto Sergeant Brice Long's desk. It was so smooth, Jace almost missed it. He grinned, knowing it wouldn't be the last time he saw the nameplate, but finally feeling at home among the Havendale police.

After pushing open the door to his office, Jace settled into his desk and reread the evidence files compiled for the deaths of both Jennifer Morris and her sister, Jasmine Hornsby. His head throbbed as he reviewed the report from Mrs. Hornsby's doctor again. With her extensive and severe arthritis, Jasmine could not have pulled the trigger of that old handgun, nor could she have reached high enough to slide the bolt which locked the door. Staring at the file, he flipped through some photos and lists of evidence they'd collected at both scenes. Not much of it did him any good.

"Well, Detective Sergeant Trueblood, from the expression on your face, I'm guessing that you're not happy with something in that report." A husky man with salt and pepper hair stood in front of the desk.

Jace nodded at Lieutenant Hank Taylor, pushing the file toward him. "You got that right, boss. I'm never happy with murder."

"Murder?" the lieutenant repeated, a hint of disquiet flashing across his face. "I thought this was a suicide case."

"That's what we were supposed to think." Jace slid the doctor's report to Taylor. "Besides this report, the forensics team noted that the blood splatter near the victim was inconsistent. There's an area on the rug that is void of blood. Something or someone was standing near the victim when the gun was fired."

"I just don't know how they locked the room after they shot her and staged the scene." He grabbed a large manila envelope and dumped out more pictures. Lining the images up across the top of his desk, he carefully scanned each colored photo. "We searched every inch of that room and found nothing: no hidden panels, no trap doors, and nothing that indicates that someone went out that upper window and locked it behind them."

Lieutenant Taylor stepped around the desk and reviewed each picture. He was halfway through the second row of photos when he tapped one of them. "That's one of those old bolts that you slide over to lock in place." Leaning closer, he asked, "Is that a piece of thread hanging there?"

"Yeah, a piece of blue silk thread," Jace slowly answered, scanning the senior officer's face. "Don't tell me that you think that thread is evidence. Does it mean something to you?"

Taylor smiled as he regarded the picture. "That, my friend, is probably the answer to your mystery of the locked door."

Jace sat back and peered at the Lieutenant curiously. Mibs Monahan had said it was important, now so did the boss. What was he missing? "Okay, I'm listening. So, what's the answer?"

"William Powell as Detective Philo Vance, in an old murder mystery movie. I think it was originally filmed in the 1940s," Taylor offered.

"What are you talking about, boss?" Jace was still confused.

"I used to watch old mystery movies with my mom and grandma when I was a kid," Taylor explained. "In one of the old movies, the killer used some combination of needles or pins and a heavy string. I think maybe it was some fishing line. Anyway, the killer hooked the string on the latch and then threaded it through the keyhole. He went out and shut the door behind him. Pulling the piece of string, he slid the latch into place. He then yanked hard enough to pull it loose and through the keyhole. I don't remember the exact details, but it was something like that."

Jace pondered this for a few moments before responding. "So, you think the killer pulled a piece of thread from outside the closed door to set the lock and make it seem like no one else had been in the room at the time of death?"

"It's possible," Taylor replied. "Thread would not be as strong as something like fishing line, so the end could have snagged and broken. Using thread could've been the killer's mistake."

Jace nodded. "Okay. If the killer made one mistake, maybe he or she made more." Leaning forward, he considered the picture again. "We just need to find another one."

Reaching for the folder with the information about the death of Jennifer Morris, Jace addressed the lieutenant. "If Jasmine Hornsby was murdered, then I think we may need to consider the possibility that the poisoned candy was actually intended for Miss Morris and not Mr. Hornsby's boss."

"Maybe," Lieutenant Taylor said, "but it doesn't

seem likely. How would James Hornsby happen to be in Conway's office at exactly the right time to be given the box of candy?" Taylor spent a few minutes flipping through the papers on Trueblood's desk. "What about the man who supposedly had the candy delivered? I understand we picked him up and charged him with suspicion of attempted murder."

"Yeah. The guy's name is Jasper Murphy," Jace answered. "He was unhappy with Bernstein Electronics, especially with Conway. Apparently, he had a very lucrative contract in the works. A few days before the agreement was signed, someone on Bernstein's board of trustees asked Conway to give the deal to another company. Conway went with what the trustee wanted. Murphy lost a huge commission, and he was furious."

"What does Murphy say?" Taylor frowned in concentration.

"He denies it, of course," Jace answered. "Claims he was home with a cold and didn't leave his apartment for two days. He insists that he didn't have anything delivered to Conway."

"Any witnesses to back his statement up?" The lieutenant stood straight with feet slightly apart, a holdover stance from when he was in the military. "Did anyone stop by? Any food deliveries?"

Jace shook his head. "Apparently not. He doesn't have an alibi *and* made a rather incriminating comment. Murphy said that it wasn't him, but he wished that whoever it was had succeeded."

"Hmm," Taylor crossed his arms. "Does James Hornsby have an alibi?"

Jace pulled out a paper from the stack on his

desk. "We have witnesses who say the box of candy was dropped off after he was already at work."

"Where was he when his wife was shot?" the lieutenant inquired.

"He was at work. Got there before eight and didn't leave until we called him about his wife's death," Jace responded.

Taylor ran his hand across his chin as he tried to remember details from the report. "Did we get any description of the person who had the box of candy delivered to the office building?"

"We interviewed the employees from the delivery company. They were so busy that morning that they don't remember much. There is a pawn shop next door with a mounted camera. We checked the footage from there and saw a person going into the delivery business at the estimated time the package was dropped off. However, he or she was wearing a long coat, hat, and sunglasses. We weren't able to see their face." Jace pulled a picture out of the pile on the desk and handed it to the lieutenant.

After studying it carefully, Hank Taylor rubbed his knuckles across his chin. "It could be anyone. The way the person is hunched over and has their head down, I can't even tell if it's a man or woman. I'd guess it's a man, but I couldn't swear to it." He handed the picture back, picked up a few others. After studying them for a few minutes, he glanced up. "Have you gone over the sisters' wills?"

"We're still waiting for the copies. There was some delay with the lawyers," Jace explained. "Are you thinking that once one sister died, someone decided to remove the other from the line of monetary succession?"

Taylor shrugged one shoulder. "It's one possibility. If so, we may have two killers."

"Let me make a call and see what's keeping those copies." Jace reached for his phone. "It'll be interesting to see who inherits all those millions. The first thought would be the husband, but with all that family money, he signed a pre-nuptial agreement. He doesn't automatically get everything, although I understand he is designated to receive a hefty amount." Jace flipped through the contacts on his iPhone, looking for the needed number. "When I interviewed the Hornsbys, the only other relative mentioned was a cousin named Francis Morris. Apparently, they only see him every few years, not too close of a relationship."

"I'm sure you'll add him to your list of people to check out." Lieutenant Taylor waved as he walked out the door. "Let me know what you find."

Chapter 9

Bernice looked at the wall clock and pushed her chair away from the desk. It was a few minutes before five. It had been a slow afternoon, but she was thankful for that. Mibs had driven over to the local high school to meet the cheer team. Her niece had been hired to make the new uniform skirts for the junior members of the group. They were slowly building clientele, which, with the proper management, would mean repeat business for years.

Bernice knew she would not be around forever, and she wanted to help as much as she could for as long as she was able. She needed to know that her girl would be all right if something happened. Bernice had been making payments on a life insurance policy for years. If the time came, it should be enough to pay off most of the mortgage on this building. Or, if Mibs preferred, it should be enough to allow her to go back to school and follow whatever dreams she may have.

Bernice's physical therapy had progressed to the point where she was out of the wheelchair. She was now getting around with the aid of a walker. She was anxious to reach the next goal, where a cane would be the only help she needed. Having assured Mibs that she could handle the shop for a couple hours by herself, the determined senior had insisted that her niece head over to the school.

She grabbed the walker and pulled herself up to a standing position. Taking a deep breath and holding the walker securely, she started toward the door.   She planned on locking it and then making a cup of tea using the hot water dispenser that Mibs had purchased for her. When she was a few feet away from the entrance, the door opened. A tall, attractive man stepped in and closed the door behind himself.

"Hello, may I help you?" Bernice asked.

The young man nodded and said, "I hope so. I'm looking for Mibs Monahan. I'm a friend of hers from college." He scanned the sewing shop. When he noticed the stairs near the back of the shop, his eyes stopped and lingered there. "Is she here? I'd like to surprise her."

"No. Mibs is out running an errand right now, but I love meeting her friends from college.   I didn't get much of a chance to go into the city and visit. I'm her Aunt Bernice." She smiled at him. "And you are?"

He gave the older woman a dismissive nod, his voice hard. "I said that I want to surprise her. When will she be back?"

A combination of the tone in the man's voice and the expression on his face sent a chill down Bernice's spine. She suddenly had an idea who he was. It had to be Nate, the young man who had been bothering Mibs before she left college. What was his last name...Nate Watson? *No. Nate Olsen. That's the name.* She knew that Mibs was scheduled to be back soon, and her first thought was to protect her niece. Staring Mr. Olsen in the eyes, she lied without one ounce of compunction. Probably wouldn't even tell Father Smith about it on Saturday at Confession. "I don't know when Mibs will be back. It will most likely be late because she is stopping at a restaurant to meet a friend for dinner."

The slightest hint of anger showed in the man's eyes as he stepped a little closer to the old woman. She could almost feel his agitation.

"Where?" he snapped. "What time was she supposed to meet this *friend*?"

Bernice tried not to flinch at his intimidating stance and demanding words. She had seen and heard a lot during her life, and a mealy-mouthed guy like this didn't intimidate her. "It's called Zachary's, and it's on the main street of town, just past the post office. She should be there soon." Bernie smiled to herself as she thought of the local bar and grill where many off-duty policemen hung out. They had great specials, and the beer was only a dollar per bottle for all veterans and first responders. Even though she knew he wouldn't find Mibs there, she decided it was an excellent place to send him.

Without another word, he turned and left the shop, the bells echoing angrily in his wake.

After he left, Bernice grumbled to herself, shaking her head, "Oh, my dear girl, I can understand why you don't want to be around that guy."

~~

A short time later, Mibs returned in a good mood. She reported to her aunt that the girls on the cheer team were great, and taking the measurements went without a problem. The club's sponsor loved the sample of sportswear material she had brought along. However, her mood quickly changed when her aunt told her of Nate's visit. Aunt Bernie insisted that she call the police and let them know that this young man had followed her to her hometown.

"I don't think the authorities will do anything. I

don't think they *can* do anything unless Olsen actually threatens or hurts me," Mibs mumbled. Yes, he had sent flowers to the shop, but she'd thought that Nate would have given up by now. It had been three dates months ago. There was nothing there; why couldn't he see that?

"Well, I don't want you to wait until a viable threat occurs," Aunt Bernie insisted. She couldn't even imagine what she'd do if something happened to Mibs. "If you call them, they will at least be aware that he is in town."

Mibs nodded. "I guess you're right."

"Of course, I'm right, young lady. I'm always right," she told her sternly, making Mibs laugh.

Hugging the older woman, her niece agreed.

"Mibs, what about that detective you met at the Hornsby home? Didn't he give you a card with his number on it?"

"Yes, but that was for information concerning the deaths of Jasmine and Jennifer." Mibs frowned as she thought about the violent loss of the two sisters. "It wasn't for my personal problems."

"Call him anyway," Aunt Bernie insisted. "Maybe he can tell you who to contact at the police station. If this Nate character goes to the pub and doesn't find you, he may come back here."

Mibs hesitated for a moment, nibbling her lip before replying. She had delayed reporting Nate Olsen before, but the thought of him possibly showing up again, especially when Aunt Bernie was alone, spurred her to action. "You may be right."

Searching her purse, she found the card that Detective Trueblood had given her.

The phone rang several times before Trueblood's

crisp voice came on the line. "Hello. Trueblood speaking."

"Detective Trueblood," she started.

"Miss Monahan? Is everything okay?"

She blinked when his voice changed from slight disinterest to complete focus.

"Umm, not totally. That's why I'm calling." Mibs paused. "I'm hoping you could tell me who to contact about...well, about a guy who persists in bothering me when I've asked him to leave me alone."

"Where are you?" his question was brusque, and she barely got the shop's name out of her mouth before he told her he would be there shortly.

Bewildered, Mibs stared at the phone. Turning to her aunt, she shook her head. "I guess we should sit down and wait."

~~

"What did he say?" Bernice asked, watching Mibs. She'd noticed the pink on the girl's cheeks and her hesitance to call the man. She hadn't met him yet, but anyone who could make her normally unflappable niece flush with just the thought of talking to him was someone Bernice needed to know.

~~

"That he was on his way," Mibs responded blankly, suddenly wondering how she looked. She had been up since five-thirty organizing the stockroom. Mibs was sure there was still a trace of spilled mustard on her shirt from a hotdog.

"I was thinking about making some tea. I'll make a cup for you, too," Aunt Bernie offered.

"Let me do it. You sit down." Mibs guided her aunt to a nearby chair and headed to the small area in the back of the shop where they kept a miniature refrigerator, microwave, and hot water maker. She needed to get her thoughts together. *Not that Jace would care*, she chided herself. He was just doing his job.

They had barely been waiting five minutes when there was a sharp rap on the door. Fearing that it would be Nate Olsen, Mibs moved toward the door and peeked out the glass insert. She relaxed when she saw it was Detective Trueblood. Opening the door, she let him in, making sure to hear the lock click in place once he was inside.

"You're here," Mibs noted inanely.

He must have been off duty. He was wearing a pair of old blue jeans with a few tears in them, spackled with dried paint. The faded and stained heather-colored t-shirt stretched snuggly across his chest. Mibs mentally scolded herself for noticing the well-defined muscles that hadn't been as apparent when he wore his suit jacket. The badge clipped to his belt and the gun holstered on his hip seemed out of place with the casual clothes.

Noticing his outfit, she stammered, "I'm...sorry. I used the number from the card you gave me. I didn't realize it would call you when you were off duty."

"It's no problem," he insisted. "I keep my work phone near me most of the time, in case of emergencies at the station. I wouldn't have given you the number if I didn't want you to use it. Besides, you sounded worried on the phone." Jace paused, studying Mibs. "So, what happened?"

~~

Jace had been busy in the past few days. They'd redoubled their efforts to check out everyone in the murdered women's lives, from the seemingly innocuous gardener who had free access to the grounds and patio to a frustrated antique dealer who coveted a few of the dolls from the sisters' collection. A few weeks ago, he would have written off someone interested in dolls; however, with the way this case was going, it seemed just as good of a lead as any. Since they were still waiting on the women's wills to see who else shook loose as a suspect, he'd decided to get a break from the investigation and work on his house for a few hours today.

Jace was standing with his hands in his pockets, listening to Mibs talk about meeting a guy named Nate in college. All of a sudden, something hard bumped his booted foot. He looked up to see an elderly woman studying him.

"You must be Detective Trueblood," the older woman offered.

He nodded, the corners of his mouth lifting in a smile. "Yes, ma'am."

"I'm Bernice, Mibs' aunt."

He offered her his hand, and Bernice took it carefully. A firm grip, but he was considerate of her fragility.

Bernice nodded, then waved toward the couch in the corner of the shop where they often had afternoon tea. "Why don't we sit down?"

~~

"Mibs has a stalker." Ignoring Mibs' protests, Bernice watched the detective. If he'd been nudged with a cattle prod, she probably wouldn't have gotten such a reaction. His entire body tensed, and the veins in his neck throbbed. Anger and determination glowed in his eyes as he went from concerned to high alert. His gaze was laser-sharp and leveled at Mibs.

~~

"For how long?" he demanded. "Do you know who it is? Has this person threatened you?"

"I told Aunt Bernie, it doesn't matter since he hasn't physically hurt me," Mibs declared. She could tell her aunt had been thoroughly charmed by the detective, even though it had only been a few seconds of conversation. Between introducing himself and now, he had done something to make her aunt beam with satisfaction.

"What?" Jace squinted at Mibs. "Of course, it matters. Someone doesn't have to hurt you to be a threat."

Mibs found herself staring at him, letting the explanation tumble from her lips. He didn't seem upset or disappointed with her. On the contrary, all she saw in those azure eyes was worry. He jotted down information as she told him about Nate. About the phone calls and notes. The unsolicited presents. The feeling that she had been followed. "All of this happened while I was at college. Why does it matter now?" she asked after talking for what seemed hours but had only been a few minutes.

~~

"It's a pattern of behavior, sweetheart." Jace snapped his mouth shut on the word, swallowing hard. Mibs seemed oblivious to his slip. He had no idea if she'd heard him or not, but he couldn't run around calling ladies sweetheart. Clearing his throat, he shifted slightly on the couch. "Anything since you've moved home?"

"That's why I made her call you," Bernice, sitting on a nearby chair, interjected. "I told her to call that detective she mentioned meeting. That you would know what to do now that Nate has shown up here in Havendale."

He flexed his jaw and growled, "He's here?"

"He sent flowers here," Bernice offered, ignoring the hesitation from Mibs.

"And he came here to the shop?" Jace asked, regarding them both seriously. Pulling out his phone, he called the station. It took him a few minutes to get hold of the sergeant on duty, but by the time he'd described the situation, Sergeant Long had promised to have a police car come by the shop in the morning.

"I'm going to have some officers come by tomorrow to talk to you," he told Mibs, waiting for her to meet his gaze. "Write down as much as you can remember. Things he said. Unwelcomed presents he sent. Any witnesses around when he's bothered you."

~~

It took a minute for Mibs to process everything he was saying. He wasn't blowing it off. Despite how frustrated she had been with him earlier in the week, she was glad he was here now. Maybe he *was* a lot nicer than his professional demeanor had suggested. After all, he had been kind when he stopped by the sewing shop after Jennifer Morris's death and friendly when they ran into each other at the café. Maybe she shouldn't be chastising herself for finding him attractive.

"If he sends anything, you keep it for evidence. If he leaves a harassing voicemail, don't erase it, and if he comes by, call me or the police. You are right that the police can't do a lot until there is a viable threat or fear of safety. If his harassment continues, you may need to go before a judge to ask for a restraining order. Any evidence or witnesses that you have could be presented to the judge to persuade him to issue it."

A few days previous, Mibs had asked her aunt about any families named Trueblood in Havendale. There had only been one, Ezekiel Trueblood, a widower for many years. After his wife, Gladys, passed away almost twenty years ago, Ezekiel stopped taking care of their home. His house had been deteriorating over time, and he'd done nothing about it. Thomas Carlyle, Ezekiel's lawyer, notified the nephew, Jace, that he had been left the property, along with a sizable monetary inheritance. Mr. Carlyle was astonished when the young detective moved to Havendale and began revamping the house.

~~

Detective Trueblood thought about what Miss Monahan had said about her relationship with this Olsen guy. It had not been significant. They hadn't been intimately involved and hadn't lived together. Jace realized that he was glad to know that fact. Why should that make him experience a sense of comfort? He stood, paced a few feet away, then stepped back.

"Are you sure you've told me everything about your time with Mr. Olsen?"

"What does that mean?" Mibs crossed her arms over her chest. For a moment, it seemed that she'd forgotten he was a cop; the concern he was displaying was because she was someone he had to protect and serve. "Do you think I did something to lead him on?" Mibs couldn't hide the hurt in her voice, even as she tried to mask it with a glare.

"No," Jace sighed, dropping back onto the couch. "I don't think you did anything wrong, Miss Monahan. I never meant to imply that."

~~

She could tell he believed her. As she searched

84

his eyes, she saw nothing but complete sincerity.

"Well," Aunt Bernie interrupted, making Mibs turn toward her aunt. "At least now, there will be a record of your complaint if this man shows up again."

"Your aunt is correct. You did the right thing reporting this. We'll be watching for Nate Olsen now, and you'll start keeping a record of everything."

Mibs nodded as Jace's eyes turned intense. "You'll call if he shows up or sends anything. We need to make sure it's all documented. No more blowing this off, Miss Monahan. In my experience, stalkers are more likely to accelerate their efforts rather than back off."

Mibs admitted to herself that she did feel better about the situation, knowing that she had people to back her up if Nate returned.

Jace gave her his personal cell number to add to the one for the station before stepping toward the door. "I guess I should get out of your way and let you two lock up."

"You certainly haven't been in the way," Aunt Bernie commented with a smile as she maneuvered her walker around. "I think I will let Mibs show you out, and I'll have another cup of tea. Thank you so much, Detective." Nodding at Mibs, the elderly woman headed toward the back room.

~~

Jace studied Mibs. She seemed calmer than she had when he'd first gotten there. He was glad he'd been at his house, stripping down the old oak doors and not at the office. His home wasn't even a five-minute drive from the shop. If he'd been at the station, it would have taken him at least fifteen minutes. All he'd had to do was rip off his gloves and grab his badge and gun before coming to Monahan's. "Your aunt seems like an extraordinary person."

Mibs smiled. "Oh, she is. She is the most important person in my life. I've always called her my aunt, but...."

~~

The expression on Jace's face showed that he was puzzled by her hesitation. "She is your aunt, isn't she?"

"Yes, technically, she's my great-aunt, but she's also legally my mother, my adoptive mother." Mibs chewed her lower lip for a moment before taking a deep breath. "Would you like to sit back down, Detective?"

"Jace," he said. "Just call me Jace," he told her with a soft smile, making Mibs swallow hard.

"Jace," she repeated cautiously. She'd thought of him as Jace but hadn't allowed herself to call him that. It seemed foolish now, trying to keep him at a distance.

Jace shrugged his shoulders. "Sure, I have a little time. To tell the truth, you've made me curious."

Facing each other across a table that served as a sewing and craft area, Jace listened while Mibs explained how her parents had died when she was just a baby. She told him that her aunt had adopted her, taken care of her, and taught her everything she knew. Mibs believed that all she had accomplished was because of her aunt's encouragement and guidance.

Mibs hadn't realized that her aunt had finished her tea and was standing nearby the table until she heard her voice.

"I could fill in some details about how I became Mirabelle's guardian, if you like."

Nodding, Jace got up and pulled a chair out for Aunt Bernie, giving her a wide smile. "I like details."

Mibs gave him an appreciative grin as her aunt settled in to explain.

~~

Bernice Monahan shared the memories of her family, her brother Henry, Mibs' parents, Marian and Ben Carpenter. And Mibs' early years.

Chapter 10

Bernice began at the beginning. "My niece Marian had a little girl, Sara. She was two years old when Marian decided that she could use a short time away from household duties and childcare. So, when her husband Ben came home on Tuesdays and Thursdays to watch Sara and start supper, Marian would join her girlfriends for an exercise class and a stop at the local coffee shop after the workout. It was just her second week enjoying her girls' night out when a pair of uniformed police officers entered the gym looking for her."

Bernice shook her head at the sad memory then continued.

"Her husband and daughter had died in a tragic fire. Afterward, Marian walked around in a daze. My brother tried to encourage her to pull herself together, but Marian felt she was to blame since she'd left them home alone. My brother tried to reassure her, but she wouldn't listen. The survivor's guilt was too great.

"For days after the deaths of her husband and child, Marian stayed in a state of shock.

"Henry moved her into her old room. It was times like those that I'm sure Henry missed his deceased wife, Nancy. Maybe she would have known what to do or say.

"Six months after the loss of Ben and Sara, Marian was going to the store and to church. She had begun to talk to her old friends. It seemed as if things were going to be all right. Then one day, she had a relapse.

"Henry and Marian were returning from the store. An ambulance sped past them and stopped at the nearby intersection. They were soon sitting among the other stopped vehicles. They were close enough to see the emergency crew pulling the victims out of the crashed cars; one of the victims was a little girl who appeared to be only two or three years old. Marian insisted that the little girl was Sara. Although Henry tried to hold onto Marian, she managed to break free, and within a matter of minutes, Henry had lost her. He approached one of the police officers who had arrived at the scene and explained about his daughter. Neither Henry nor the police had found her by the time the accident scene was cleared away. He decided to go home and see if Marian had returned, but she wasn't there. It wasn't until two days later that Marian was found sleeping on a bench in the local train station.

"That was the first time she ran off. After that, Henry was afraid to leave her alone, even to run a short errand. He called me and asked for help. So I would stay with Marian from time to time, giving Henry an occasional break. Days would go by when Marian seemed fine. Then, something would happen, and she would wander off. Henry would find her usually within a few hours, but sometimes it would be days before he saw her wandering the streets. One time, he got a call from the police two towns away. Marian had climbed on a bus. When the bus driver realized that she didn't have a ticket, he had her get off at the next stop. Fortunately, the driver sensed that something was wrong with her and called the police. When they showed up, she asked them to call her dad, rattling off his phone number.

"Two years after Marian had returned to live with him, Henry found out that he had cancer. It was in an advanced stage, and he didn't have much time left. My brother was a strong man of faith, so he wasn't afraid of dying. He called me and said, 'Bernie, I know you were planning on coming this weekend, but could you come sooner, like today or tomorrow?'

"I could tell by his voice that he needed me there. I didn't hesitate and told him I'd come over a little past five o'clock.

"After supper, Marian went to her room to read. Henry and I sat on the glider swing on the front porch and watched the on-and-off sparkle of the fireflies across the lawn. After learning of my brother's illness, I just clutched his arm and leaned against his shoulder. Nothing was said for quite a while.

"'Finally', I declared, 'We can fight this. We will find the best cancer doctors and the best treatments ...'

"But Henry interrupted me. 'It's already gone too far. My kidneys are starting to shut down. The doctors give me about a year; maybe a little more or a little less. Bernie, I'm not worried about me. I'm not scared of dying. But the thing that is worrying me...well...'

"'Yes,'" I said, 'I'll do it.' Squeezing his arm tighter, I assured him, 'I'll take care of Marian.'

"I made plans to close my sewing shop, Monahan's Fine Sewing and Dressmaking. It had become time to put aside the demands of a business and focus on my brother and niece's needs.

"Three months later, I had gotten my affairs in

order and moved into my brother's home. Six weeks after that, Marian wandered off again. We canvased the neighborhood and all the places where they had found her before. The police were called. Friends helped search for days. Between cancer and the hunt for Marian, Henry was overcome with exhaustion and ended up in bed for two weeks. Days turned to weeks and then to months. Henry and I slowly began to lose hope of ever seeing Marian again."

Bernice paused for a moment as she recalled old memories. Rubbing her forehead, she continued.

"It was almost a year later when Henry received a call about Marian. From what Sister Mary Rose from St. Martin's Shelter said and Marian's comments after they finally got her home, Henry and I pieced together what we believe had happened to her.

"When a bus heading north pulled out of Havendale, no one noticed the woman sleeping in a seat in the back. When the bus reached its final stop, the bustling city of Metrofield, the bus driver made one last sweep to check for any left items. That's when he found her and tried to wake her. All Marian could say was, 'I lost Sara; I can't find Sara.'"

Chapter 11

Bernice continued. "It didn't take long for the other homeless people in the city to begin recognizing Marian.

"Marian first showed up at the soup kitchen. Maybe hunger drew her to the smell of cooking food, or perhaps, someone directed her to St. Martin's. For the most part, the people ignored her. She became known by some of the regular patrons of St. Martin's as the *doll lady* when she found a discarded baby doll somewhere and spent hours rocking and talking to 'her baby.'"

Bernice sighed as she remembered a woman her niece had mentioned a few times after they'd brought Marian back home.

"An older lady named Doris had been on the streets for years. She took the doll lady under her wing. Doris probably saved Marian's life by teaching her to find food and other items, showing her the places to go, and the places to avoid. She got Marian to say what her name was and that she was searching for her husband and her baby girl. Over time, Marian learned to survive on the street as she continued the quest, in her mind, of finding Sara and Ben.

"My brother had become so weak that he had to use a walker to get around and spent most of his time in bed or dozing in the living room recliner.

"One day, the phone rang, and we were both so relieved to find out that they had found Marian. But we couldn't believe it when they told me she had a baby.

"She was found at a homeless shelter that local religious sisters were running. When the sister saw Marian trying to give the baby some milk, she thought it was a doll. When she realized it was actually a baby, she sat down and got her to talk. After discussing what a baby needs, Sister Mary Rose suggested taking the baby to a doctor for a check-up. That's when Marian said not to worry because Dr. Shoemaker would see Sara if she needed a doctor. Sister asked if she knew the doctor's number in case anyone else wanted to call him. Marian said that her father would know his number. She gave the nun Henry's name and phone number. The sister wrote it down and called to see if we knew her. When she described her, I was reasonably sure that it was Marian. When she called her baby Sara, well...we knew it must be Marian.

"We wondered about the baby and had no idea who the father could be. And, well, I had never raised a little one before. Neither of us was young anymore.

"Henry kept worrying about putting all this extra work on me, but I assured him that I don't do anything unless I darn well want to. I told him that if I found I couldn't take care of her, of all of them, by myself, then I'd get the help I needed.

"The trip to Metrofield went smoothly. I'd bought an infant car seat, purchased two bottles of formula and a package of disposable diapers for the ride home.

"When I reached St. Martin's, Sister Mary Rose was waiting for me. The sister checked my identification before she handed me a gallon zip-lock bag with a little pink outfit inside. She explained, 'This belongs to the baby. It was soaked through when I bathed her last night, so I found a one-piece pajama that fit. I ran this romper through the washer and dryer.' She told me that one of the assistants helped her coax Marian into taking a shower and brushing her teeth. Her clothes were so worn out that they threw them away and found her a new outfit from their clothing cabinet.

"I thanked the sister for her kindness, and then she led me into the room where Marian was sitting with the baby in her arms.

"As soon as Marian saw me, she smiled and asked me if I wanted to hold the little one. Marian didn't seem to realize that she had been gone from home for over a year.

"Doctor Shoemaker, a long-time friend to Henry, was waiting at the house when I returned that evening with Marian and the baby. He stayed for several hours. Before he left, the doctor let Henry know that his daughter was malnourished and dehydrated, but unless the blood test showed some illness or adverse condition, she should recover with care and adequate food. The baby, to his surprise, was in remarkably good shape. We concluded that Marian must have spent all her resources on taking care of the little girl instead of herself.

"I heard Henry ask Doctor Shoemaker if Marian had talked about the circumstances of the birth. The doctor replied that Marian had mumbled something about a woman named Doris helping her."

Bernice hesitated; sadness mixed with anger flickered across her face before she continued the story.

"We believed that a man took advantage of my

niece and got her pregnant. I realized that we'd likely never know the name of the baby's father.

"The doctor assisted us in getting a birth certificate, and Henry and I chose Mirabelle Louise, our mother's name, for the baby.

"Later that year, I buried my brother. I had become a mother to a six-month-old baby and guardian of my niece. I adopted the baby, with the doctor's help, and had my great-niece baptized at Christ the King Church with her new legal name, Mirabelle Louise Monahan. Marian and little Mibs, as we called her, both thrived. Having the baby to take care of seemed to stabilize Marian. Still, I took extra precautions like the unique alarm bracelets I put on my niece and my great-niece. I also had an alarm system installed on the doors in case Marian tried to go outside during the night. Despite my precautions, I couldn't have prevented the incident that left me as my great-niece's sole support and guardian.

"We'd taken a walk in the park and stopped to rest on a wooden bench. Two-and-a-half-year-old Mirabelle had fallen asleep, napping quietly in her stroller. Marian closed her eyes and seemed to be relaxing. So, I pulled out a magazine from my bag.

"Several minutes later, hearing Marian's voice, I glanced up from the magazine to see my niece walking toward the street. On the other side of the road, a curly-haired little girl was walking with her father.

"Marian was calling for Sara and Ben, and she was so focused on the little girl and man her mind saw as her deceased family that she didn't realize what she was doing. She stepped into the street right in front of oncoming traffic. I screamed at the same time the tires screeched.

"A few days later, I told little Mibs that 'it's just you and me now. I'll try my best to take care of you. I'll make sure you get good food and go to school. I'll make sure you have decent clothing.'

"I noticed that the pair of slacks on Mirabelle was getting short and told her, 'Well, that's one thing I can definitely do. I can make you all the clothes that you need. They didn't call me the best seamstress in two counties for nothing. Maybe when you get older, I can teach you how to sew.'

"I remember hugging Mibs tightly and promising her that I would give her the best childhood I could."

Chapter 12

Aunt Bernie ended her story with a faraway expression on her face. She seemed to be remembering each detail of what happened so many years ago.

Mibs gently squeezed her aunt's age-speckled hand. "That's how I became Mirabelle Monahan and ended up with the best mother I could ever ask for."

Jace had heard many things over the years and wasn't easily stunned. But he was astonished by this story, thinking of the years of love and sacrifice Bernice Monahan had given to her niece. And how, despite the circumstances of her childhood, Mibs had become this fantastic woman.

"So," Jace hesitated as he searched for the right words. "You know all about this, Mibs? Your mother's breakdown after her husband and first daughter died, the fact that you never knew your father?"

~~

Misty-eyed, Mibs slowly nodded. "Yes." Gazing lovingly at her aunt, she continued, "I knew from an early age that my mother had died when she was hit by a car. Aunt Bernie told me that my mom's husband had died in a fire. It wasn't until I was around twelve years old that I began wondering about things. I had been paging through an old family album and asked Aunt Bernie why I was the only one in the family that has light, red-blond hair. Everyone else has darker hair and a sturdier build. It also dawned on me that my aunt always said, 'your mom's husband.' She never called him my dad."

Aunt Bernie sighed. "I had pointed out Marian and Ben in several of the pictures in the album. Then Mibs tapped on one of the pictures and asked who the little girl was on her mom's lap. I decided that it would be better to tell her the truth that it was her half-sister who had died in the same fire as Ben. I decided that if I didn't tell her, she would become even more curious as she got older."

"I'm glad she did," Mibs said. "At first, it was a lot to take in and understand. I struggled with what I had learned, but in the end, I was glad I knew the truth." Leaning toward her aunt, Mibs added, "I accepted that what happened couldn't be changed. What I realized most was that I had Aunt Bernie's unconditional love and that she had given me a good life. I was, and still am, an incredibly lucky person."

"Oh, Mibs, you have been the best part of my life," Aunt Bernie responded with a catch in her voice. Patting the tears from her eyes and taking a moment to compose herself before grabbing her walker to get up, the old woman sighed. "I think I'll go to my room now." Turning to Detective Trueblood, she nodded. "Thanks for listening to the reminiscence of an old woman."

Jace stood up and helped Bernice as she steadied herself on the walker. "Thank you for sharing your memories with me."

After the door closed to Aunt Bernie's room, Jace cleared his throat. "You've been fortunate to have her in your life."

Mibs stood and nodded as she contemplated the self-assured man who had leaned forward as they talked. A subtle scent of spicy aftershave filled the air, and a lock of hair had slipped across his forehead. Mibs had a sudden temptation to brush the wayward chestnut curl back in place. Instead, she kept her hand at her side. "Aunt Bernie and I make a good team."

His lips turned up, suggesting a smile. "Does your aunt share your interest in trying to solve mysteries?"

Is he teasing me? "Well, hmm, well, I wasn't trying to interfere." At the thought of the deaths of that fine woman and her sister, a lump formed in her throat. She swallowed and took a deep breath. "I just knew that Jasmine wouldn't kill herself. Despite her physical weakness, she was a very strong-willed person."

"It's okay," Jace said. "I believe you. There are too many inconsistencies to accept the suicide explanation."

Raising her eyebrows, Mibs asked, "Really? What inconsistencies? Did you find another way out of the room?"

Jace chuckled. "Now, now, Miss Marple, I need you to focus on documenting your stalker, not trying to do a job I'm paid by the city to do."

Mibs nodded.

The white of his teeth flashed before he shook his head slowly.

~~

"What is it about you?" he asked softly before explaining what his lieutenant had come up with about the door and the thread. He also told her that he wondered if the deaths of the two sisters might be related.

"I've said more than I should already." He stopped to consider the woman gazing up at him.

"For some reason, I find it very easy to talk to you."

Mibs shyly glanced away. "I don't mind talking to you either, Jace."

"Okay, good." Jace ran his hand through his hair, searching for the right words to say. "All right, Mibs. I guess I better get going."

Mibs walked him to the door. "Please, let me know if you find out what happened to Jasmine and Jennifer. They were such nice ladies. I don't understand why anyone would've wanted to hurt them."

"I'll do my best to find out the answers to those questions." Jace hesitated in the doorway. "You have my numbers; I expect you to call me if anything happens with Olsen."

Mibs nodded.

"I mean it, Mibs," he insisted. Suddenly tongue-tied, Jace paused. Then he softly added, "You can call me, even if it's not about him. If you want."

~~

Mibs smiled, his concern for her and his consideration for her aunt making her feel bold. "You have my number, too, Jace." Giving herself a second to change her mind, Mibs leaned against the door. "You can call me if you want."

Jace nodded, a grin lighting his face. "Duly noted. Goodnight, Mibs."

"Goodnight, Jace."

When he was gone, Mibs checked to see that all the doors and windows were locked. Then, she knocked on Aunt Bernie's door. As soon as her aunt answered, Mibs stuck her head into the room, suggesting they order pizza and just relax for the evening.

Aunt Bernie agreed wholeheartedly. "By the

way, how many days is your friend, Whitney, planning on staying during Thanksgiving vacation?"

"She'll be here Friday evening through Sunday. Her parents insisted that she spend Thanksgiving Day with them, and her mom wants her to hit a bunch of super sales on Friday morning before she leaves. It will be so good to catch up!" Mibs beamed at the thought of seeing her former roommate again.

"And the detective, did he leave in good spirits?" Aunt Bernie teased, laughing as Mibs shook her head. "He seems lovely!"

Mibs shut the door loudly, declaring she was ordering the pizza and couldn't hear her.

Chapter 13

Jace and his fellow detective, Juan Mendoza, entered a modern-style building featuring numerous oversized windows and doors. The two men stepped into the elevator, and Juan pushed the up button. When they exited, they were facing large windows that extended the length of the hallway. The interior design mimicked the open view of the exterior, giving clear sight of the sidewalk and street below. *How ironic to have an open floor plan where everyone could see in and out, yet the same building could be cloaking a murderer's secret.* To the left of the elevators and across from the windows, a sign with the word RECEPTION in block letters stared back at them. They pulled open the double glass doors and entered an area tastefully decorated in neutral tones. Several obviously expensive paintings hung on three walls, and half a dozen well-padded chairs were arranged in front of a wooden counter.

A middle-aged woman with short, wavy hair glanced up from the folder she was reading. The name on the plaque in front of her read *Cindy Wills*. "May I help you, gentlemen?" she closed the folder and stacked it on a pile of papers on the counter.

Detective Trueblood presented his badge and explained that Mr. Conway was expecting them.

"I'll let his secretary know you're here and have one of the aides escort you to his office." The receptionist reached for an older-style interoffice phone.

"Before you do that, we would like to speak to you, Ms. Wills," Juan Mendoza said.

The receptionist removed her hand from the phone and sat back in her chair. "Oh, okay. What do you need to know?"

"I believe you were the person who took the box of chocolate-covered peanuts to Mr. Conway's office the day before Mr. Hornsby's wife died. Is that correct?"

Clearing her throat, Cindy quietly responded, "Yes, I did." The color drained from her face as she quickly added, "But I had no idea there was a problem! It was brought in by a service that had delivered items before. None of the aides were handy, so I... took it to uh...Helen, Mr. Conway's secretary, myself." The woman's hands shook, and her voice trembled.

Hoping to put her at ease, Jace said in a reassuring tone, "That's fine, Ms. Wills. We have all that in our report. We're talking to several people again just in case they remembered something they hadn't thought of when they were first interviewed."

Cindy let out a long breath.

Detective Mendoza pulled a small notebook from his pocket and flipped the pages. "Ma'am, according to my notes, you told the officer who previously interviewed you that James Hornsby came through the lobby before the delivery was made. Is that correct?"

"Yes." She nodded. "He walked by and headed down the hall before the delivery boy brought the box to the counter."

"Did the delivery person say anything when he handed you the box?"

"Only that he had a delivery for Conway. Then

he asked me to sign when I accepted." Cindy tapped her chin as she tried to remember. "I'm sure that's all."

Mendoza closed his notebook and stuck it back in his pocket. "Thank you, ma'am. If you think of anything else, please give us a call."

She smiled at the two detectives and picked up the phone to call Mr. Conway's office. Then, the receptionist added, "You know, it is kind of interesting. If Mr. Hornsby had stayed out in the entranceway any longer, he wouldn't have been heading down the hall before that box was delivered. He would have walked in at the same time."

Jace froze in place for a second before turning toward the doors they had come through. They had a clear view through the glass doors.

"Ms. Wills, what do you mean that Mr. Hornsby stayed in the entranceway?"

"What?" she responded.

"You mentioned that Mr. Hornsby didn't come in immediately. How long did he linger in the hall? Was he doing something or just standing there?"

Cindy rolled her eyes to the ceiling in thinking mode. "How long?" She paused. "Oh, not too long, maybe two or three minutes, I guess."

"What was he doing?" Jace repeated. "Was he looking at something or someone?"

She shrugged. "I'm not sure. I didn't pay that much attention." Cindy sat back and then leaned forward again. "I think he did peer through the outside windows a few times."

"And James Hornsby didn't say anything to you when he went by?" Mendoza asked.

"No, he didn't say a word." Hands shaking again, Cindy said, "Did I say something wrong?

What does Mr. Hornsby taking a few minutes to come in have to do with anything?"

With a wave of dismissal, Jace said, "It probably doesn't mean anything. We just like to have all the facts, no matter how unimportant they seem."

A few minutes later, the two detectives were sitting in Mr. Conway's office.

Conway leaned back against his chair and frowned. "So, you think Jasper Murphy tried to poison me? I knew he was upset but never imagined something like this."

"He is our prime suspect, but we don't have enough proof to formally charge him," Detective Mendoza explained. "We're still reviewing evidence."

"Not enough proof?" Conway questioned. "The card said it was from him. Isn't that enough?"

Juan Mendoza cut his eyes over to the senior detective and raised an eyebrow.

Jace understood that he was asking permission to give some information. He nodded.

"The problem is," Juan explained, "the card was typed, not handwritten. If that's all we have, Murphy's lawyer will make the case that anyone could have given his name and had the package sent."

A flicker of fear shone in Conway's eyes for a moment. "If he's released, will he make another attempt? Should I be worried?"

"Like I said, we're still reviewing evidence," Juan reassured him. "We'll let you know what develops."

Detective Trueblood ran his hand through his hair and leaned forward. "Would you tell us again how it happened that James Hornsby ended up taking the box of chocolates home? Who suggested that he do that?"

"Well," Conway thought for a moment, "I told him he should take them home for his sister-in-law because I couldn't eat them. I'm allergic to nuts, so unless I had my secretary take them to the company break room, they would've gone to waste. Having James take them home seemed like a good idea."

"Okay, Mr. Conway. But how did you know that his sister-in-law would like them?"

"Hmm, let me think. I remember that Hornsby commented on how nice it was that someone sent a gift, and I said something along the lines that the sales rep was probably trying to sway me toward giving him a contract. I don't remember the exact words. That's when I said the candy would be wasted on me because I couldn't eat peanuts."

"Go on, Mr. Conway. What was said after that?"

"He mentioned that his wife likes soft-centered chocolates, and his sister-in-law likes candy with a crunch. That's when I suggested that he take the box of chocolate-covered peanuts home." Mr. Conway sat forward and drummed his fingers on the desk. "Why are you asking about Hornsby? Are you implying that he planned to have me give him the candy all along?"

"Mr. Conway, as I said, we're not suggesting anything. We're just gathering information," Jace assured him.

"Okay, well, good." Conway sat back in his oversized office chair and muttered, "Hornsby has worked for me for almost ten years. I've never had a problem with his work."

Standing, the senior detective added, "We'll let you know if we have any more questions."

As they left the building, Mendoza turned to Trueblood. "I'm beginning to think we should give Hornsby a closer review."

"I agree, but we shouldn't jump to any conclusions. Everything we heard could be nothing more than coincidence," Jace said. "Remember, James Hornsby has an alibi for both the time of Jennifer Morris's death and his wife's death."

"That's true, but it still makes me wonder. Maybe we should double-check those alibis," Mendoza suggested.

"It wouldn't hurt." Jace tilted his head, heading toward the car. "But don't stop checking on Murphy. Check any local store that sells that specific box of candy. Someone somewhere should have seen something. For now, I reckon we need ta git back to the station. They should have delivered copies of the wills by now. I want to see exactly who inherits from the two sisters. We need to find out the person or persons who benefit from their deaths."

Chapter 14

Back in his office, Detective Trueblood sat down at his desk and passed a copy of Jennifer Morris's will to Juan Mendoza. "Pull up a chair, Juan. You can read that while I scan this copy of Jasmine Hornsby's will."

Both detectives were scribbling notes as they read through the documents. Half an hour later, Juan sat back and reread his summary of the Morris will.

"Wow! These ladies had quite a lot of money and numerous stocks and investments," he exclaimed.

"Yep. These women were extremely well-off," Jace agreed. "It appears that they were pretty generous in their wills, but then again, they could afford to be." The detective stretched his neck muscles and flexed his shoulders to work out the kinks that had developed from leaning over the desk. "Did you find anything worth noting?"

"She left a $1,000 bonus for the gardener and another thousand for a monthly cleaning crew. There's a donation of $500,000 to a local church. That's half a million. We can check it out, but I doubt we'd find anything there. She has six different charities listed that get a hundred thousand each. They are well-known foundations. Again, we could check them out, but we'd probably be wasting our time." Juan paused as he read the next note. "Hmm, she left a half-million to someone named Jane de Bois." Glancing across the desk at Jace, he asked. "Do you know who that is?"

"That's the housekeeper, Janie," he nodded.

Juan arched his eyebrows. "That's a lot of money to leave a housekeeper, isn't it?"

"Yes and no." Jace made a back and forth motion with his hand. "Five-hundred thousand would be a whole lot for most people, but Morris and Hornsby had a combined worth of over $100 million. Jane de Bois has been working for them for years, and I got the impression that the two sisters were very fond of her." He ran his hand through his hair, then added, "We can recheck her, but I had a pretty thorough investigation done already. We didn't find anything that would make me consider her a serious suspect. But..."

"But," Juan questioned, "we'll check again?"

"Always double-check everything." Jace nodded. "What else does the will say?"

"Francis Morris inherits $1 million. I have our new detective, Delgado, examining his background and doing a check on his movements these last few weeks." Taking a deep breath, Juan continued, "After that, simply put, it states that if Jennifer precedes her sister, Jasmine Morris Hornsby, in death, then Jasmine gets the remainder of everything that's left. If her sister had died first, then the bulk of the Morris estate would have gone towards establishing a trust that will distribute funds to various scholarships for the local schools and improvements for the Havendale park districts."

"So," Jace leaned back in his chair and propped his polished, leather shoe up on the edge of the desk. "The fact that Jennifer passed away first meant that pretty much everything went to Jasmine. Which makes the death of Jasmine Hornsby a few weeks later even more substantial."

"I still think James Hornsby is at the top of the list as a suspect!" Juan sounded frustrated. "We need to see if his alibis are really as solid as they seem."

Jace paused. "Or someone is setting it up to seem like that." Smiling at his fellow detective, he picked up the copy of the Hornsby will. "The thing is that James Hornsby doesn't inherit everything. He *only* gets $5 million." Jace put his foot down and straightened his chair. "The rest of the will is set up pretty much like her sister's. Monetary gifts to the household help, the church, and listed charities. One million to the cousin. Five million to the husband. The rest would go to Jennifer if she were the survivor of the two sisters, or into scholarships and trusts if her sister were already gone."

"Okay. Still, $5 million is a lot of money. More than I'll ever see in my lifetime. More than most people will ever have at one time." Lifting his right shoulder in a half-shrug, he added, "Of course, one million is more than enough motive for some people."

"You're right about that, Juan. People have been murdered for much less. Let me know as soon as we get the report on Francis Morris. As far as James Hornsby, who knows? Maybe he plans on contesting the will and trying to get the complete estate?" Jace speculated. "Or maybe he resented the fact that his wife and her sister held the financial strings in the household, and he was tired of waiting to be a millionaire. Or maybe Hornsby is just a grieving husband." Sighing, he shook his head. "Too many 'ors,' Juan. Too many maybes and too many unanswered questions." Turning a page of the Hornsby will, Jace pondered,

"Does it say anything about who all gits the doll collection?" As the day drew on, Jace's southern accent began slipping into his conversation.

Juan nodded. "It did, but I guess I didn't think it was that important. Is there something special about these dolls?"

"I've been doing a little research. Apparently, some collectible dolls are worth more than I realized. I don't know if there are many in this collection, but I don't want to totally ignore them." He compared the information on the two wills. "They both list the same museum as the recipient of any of the dolls that the curator would like to add to the museum's inventory. It states that any dolls left after the museum selects what they want are to be sold, and the proceeds will go to the children's wing of the local hospital."

"I doubt that the collection has anything to do with the murders," Juan said.

Jace agreed with him but added, "The housekeeper, Janie, did mention that there is an antique collector who tried several times to get the sisters to sell a #1 Vintage Barbie doll, but they wouldn't part with it. I guess it is valuable. I interviewed the guy, William Jensen. He seemed a bit fanatical about his antiques but not enough to lead to murder."

"I'll have him checked out again," Juan said, "just to cover all the bases."

Jace glanced at the old, white-faced clock on the wall and listened to the metallic click-click of the second hand for a few moments. Tossing the document on his desk, he suggested, "Let's take a break and get some lunch."

"You don't have to tell me twice." Juan reached for his jacket.

Just as the two men stood to leave the room, Sergeant Long strolled to the office door. After taking the toothpick out of his mouth, the tall, lean officer announced, "Macey Buckmore is here and wants to talk to you. He says it's about the Hornsby case."

Jace frowned, perplexed. "Do we know this Macey Buckmore?"

"Oh yeah, we know him," Long replied. "Ask Mendoza. He can tell you all about good ol' Macey. I'll send him in and let you talk to him. I have thick pastrami on rye waiting for me that's a lot more appealing than another one of his theories." Sergeant Long gave a short salute and walked back to the entrance desk.

Juan Mendoza blew out a breath. "Macey advertises himself as Havendale's best private detective. As far as I know, he is the *only* PI in the area. He comes in here every few months with another theory on solving a local crime. Usually, it's a cold case that no one has thought about in years. As far as I know, his 'tips,' 'theories,' whatever you want to call them, never lead anywhere." Juan paused. "Wait! I take that back. There was one time he did have actual information. He was sneaking around the strip mall late in the evening, snapping pictures of the manager from the hearing aid store. The guy's wife was sure he was having an affair with the realtor from the building next door. When Macey developed the photos he had taken, one of them had a background shot of someone breaking into a car. We'd had a series of thefts from cars in that area at that time. I have to say, Buckmore does take good, clear pictures, and we were able to use the snapshots to find the guy along with a number of the stolen items." Juan lifted his hands palms up and shrugged. "But most of his tips are more along the line of conspiracy theories."

Jace nodded just as Macey Buckmore reached the office doorway. As the man entered the room, he removed his buff, gray cowboy hat and held out his hand. Jace accepted Buckmore's beefy handshake.

"Hello, Mr. Buckmore. I'm Detective Jace Trueblood. I understand that you may have some information for us."

When they shook hands, Jace noted that the private investigator had on high-heeled, leather boots tooled with intricate cactus designs. The western-style shirt sported a bolo tie with a turquoise stone insert and metal pointed collar tips. A round face and round belly indicated that he enjoyed eating, and Jace wondered if the too white, too-straight teeth were original or if there had been a point in the man's past when he'd lost his teeth and needed replacements.

"Call me Macey!" Buckmore's voice boomed in the small room. "Nice to see that the town has added some new blood to the police force. How 'bout I call you Jace?"

Wanting to start off on a more professional level, Jace replied, "You can call me Detective Trueblood or just Detective will be fine." Jace usually preferred that title rather than a more formal one of First Sergeant or Chief of Detectives.

"Sure, sure!" Macey grinned widely.

Gesturing to the chair that the other detective had just vacated, Jace said, "Please, sit down, Mr. Buckmore." As Jace walked back around the desk to reclaim his seat, Juan leaned against the wall, folding his arms across his chest.

Jace said, "I understand that y'all have some information to share with us about the death of Mrs. Hornsby?"

"I sure as heck do!" Buckmore declared. "*I* know who killed her. Her sister, too."

Chapter 15

Mibs folded the baby quilt and placed it in the flat, white box that she had lined with tissue paper. She added tissue over the quilt and put the lid on. Mrs. Miner had brought in clothing for alterations when Monahan's Sewing Shop first opened. She had since ordered several custom-made jackets and, two months ago, had requested a handmade quilt for her first grandchild due in a few weeks. Mrs. Miner had wanted a baby blanket, a replica of one that had belonged to her mother. The old sample showing a tumbling block pattern hinted at previously vibrant, primary colors now faded over the years. Since the grandmother-to-be had wanted it hand-sewn instead of on the sewing machine, the project had taken Mibs a bit longer than she had planned. But it had turned out beautifully! Mrs. Miner should come tomorrow to claim her special gift.

While she was working on the baby quilt, Mibs had decided to research the possibility of adding sewing and quilting lessons to the shop's list of services. That would mean giving up a couple evenings each week, but she felt it would be an enjoyable source of increased income.

Mibs turned to her aunt, who sat behind the counter, reading the latest *Spools and Thimbles* publication. "Aunt Bernie, what would you think if I set aside two hours on Monday and Wednesday evenings for sewing classes? I'm thinking of beginning sewing lessons on one day and quilting classes on the other day."

"Hmm," Aunt Bernie mumbled as she turned a page in the magazine. "You put in a lot of long hours already. I wouldn't want you to overdo things." Aunt Bernie sat the periodical aside and looked at her niece. "But it's something I know you could do. Would you be doing it for the money or because you want to share the enjoyment you get out of making something new from materials?"

"A bit of both," Mibs answered. "Mending and altering clothing is a job I can do well, but it's still a job. On the other hand, when I make something new, it feels more like I'm creating a piece of artwork." Mibs thought about her love of finishing a project and seeing it turn out well. Maybe it was the same feeling a sculptor had when he or she created a statue or art piece. "Even though it was time-consuming, I was happy to make the baby quilt that I just finished. When I made a homecoming dress, I tried to create a unique design, making it special for each girl. I would picture in my mind how the young lady would feel in the dress as she walked to the dance floor."

Mibs set the box for Mrs. Miner on a shelf behind the counter. After turning to her aunt, she gave her a hug and said, "Even though it has been a lot of work opening our shop, I'm glad we did it. I know things will be tight for several years, but I think we can handle it." Pausing to gauge her aunt's sentiment, she asked, "Aunt Bernie, how do you feel now that we've been open for a while?"

Smiling, Aunt Bernie answered, "I think we can do anything if we make a decision, take that first step, and don't stop until we've accomplished our goal." The old woman patted Mibs on the arm. "I also think that your sewing classes would be a good idea. Let's plan when you want to start these lessons, so we can put an advertisement in the paper."

Mibs grabbed the folder that she used to jot down notes and sat down next to her aunt. "Well, let's see. I thought that I could put up a couple of tables in the corner by the back staircase. I'll need to rearrange some of the displays. Oh, and I'll need to set up a couple more sewing machines." Putting her hands on the sides of her face, she leaned forward. "Hmm, more sewing machines. That would be an added expense."

"Hey, they don't have to be new or fancy. To begin with, you'll only need ones that have basic stitches," Aunt Bernie said. "Do you remember the two older machines that are stored in the back? I used them for years, and they were always dependable. Do you know somewhere nearby where we can have them cleaned, checked out, and oiled?"

"When I go over to the community theater, I pass a shop on Third Street that does various kinds of repairs. Let me think. The sign stenciled across their window says Tony's something. I think it says, 'Tony's Vintage Treasures and Fix-It Shop.' I could stop and see if he repairs sewing machines. Maybe he has some used ones to sell."

"Vintage Treasures? That sounds interesting. Maybe I'll go with you if you don't mind." Aunt Bernie rubbed her leg. "I'm trying to get short bouts of exercise to strengthen my leg muscles."

"Sure," Mibs readily agreed. "We should take a long lunch tomorrow. We could go to the 'Fix-it' shop and then stop for a bite to eat."

Mibs and her aunt turned toward the door when they heard the bells jingling. Mibs shivered when Nate Olsen swaggered through the doorway, holding a colorful bouquet of mixed flowers in his arm.

"Mibs!" Nate beamed. "You're still here. I passed by earlier and saw you through the window. I was afraid you might've left before I got back. But I wanted to get some flowers for you." Holding the bundle out, he moved toward the counter. "I've missed you so much!"

When Mibs didn't respond, he stepped closer and placed the floral arrangement on the counter. The scent of roses, lilies, dahlias, and baby's breath spread across the area.

"These are for you, Mibs." Nate reached for her hand.

She pulled away. "What are you doing here, Nate? I told you I didn't want to see you again."

The smug expression seeping across Nate's face made it clear that her words were falling on deaf ears. "You don't mean that. I know how women play hard to get. *You* expect *me* to pursue you." A sudden spark of anger flickered in his eyes as he glared at her. "But, come on, Mibs! You're a little ridiculous! Stop playing games, and let me take you out tonight."

Nate seemed so intent on watching Mibs that he didn't notice when Aunt Bernie picked up her phone. A few seconds later, Jace's voice came through the telephone.

"Trueblood here. How can I help you?"

"Who's that?" Nate yelled. "Hang up the phone!"

Aunt Bernie glared back at the irritating man but did not move.

Jace's voice could be heard again. "Mibs? Is that you? Is that man there? Mibs?"

"I said to hang up, old woman!" As he reached toward her aunt, Mibs hit him with her notebook.

118

"Get out of here, Nate! My aunt called the police, and they'll be here any minute. Go away and don't come back!"

The hateful glare on Nate Olsen's face made Mibs flinch and lean away.

"You'll be sorry you ever teased me, playing your games." Heading toward the door, Nate peered over his shoulder and hissed, "You'll be sorry!"

A few minutes later, a police car pulled up in front of the shop. Two officers got out and hurried through the doorway. "We had a call about a disturbance here. What's wrong?"

With a shaky voice, Mibs responded, "He left when he found out the police were on their way."

"Officer," Aunt Bernie interrupted, "there is someone from the police station who wants to talk to you." She had never hung up the phone, hoping that Jace or someone at the police station had been listening to Nate's threatening words. After the stalker left, Bernie spoke on the phone, grateful to hear a response.

The officer accepted the cell phone from Aunt Bernie. He listened and said, "Detective Trueblood is on his way."

~~

A short time later, Jace rushed in, hurrying over to Mibs and Bernie. "Are you two all right?"

As Bernie nodded, a stern focus spread across her features. Jace had a feeling that she would never have let Olsen see her cower, even if the police hadn't shown up.

Mibs stepped around the counter and faced Jace. "Thank you for coming," she whispered, her whole body trembling.

After a slight hesitation, the detective wrapped

119

his arm around her, taking his first real breath since picking up the phone at the station. "It's okay, now. You're okay."

The police officers took notes. They assured the two women a patrol car would drive by the shop every few hours for the rest of the night.

"Do you have a picture of this guy, Olsen?" asked the officer. "We have his description, but a picture would be better."

"I don't personally have a picture of him, but there should be one in our college yearbook," Mibs answered. "Will that work?"

"Yes, ma'am, we could make a copy from that."

Mibs went upstairs to find the yearbook. While she was up there, Jace talked with Bernie to make sure the older woman was indeed all right.

"I'm fine. Just keep that guy away from my girl!"

Jace grinned at the octogenarian's tenacity. "Yes, ma'am. I'll do my best."

Mibs returned with the book and handed it to the police officers who took it and the flowers with them.

Jace convinced Mibs to fill out a request for a restraining order. He told her that once he heard the voices on the phone, he started recording the call. He had another detective continue to monitor the call while he hurried over to the sewing shop. With the recording and their testimony, the judge would most likely issue the order. Mibs walked with him to the door.

"Make sure to check the locks after I leave," he cautioned.

"Thank you again, Jace." Mibs gazed at him, smiling.

Jace struggled to pull himself away. His heart raced at the thought of Mibs being hurt. *What is it about this girl?*

"I need to stop beating around the bush and just ask you."

Mibs hesitated. "Ask me what?"

"Will you go to dinner with me, Mibs?" Jace was seldom shy with women, but around this young lady, he suddenly felt nervous.

~~

Mibs considered Jace attractive, but there had been a couple times she had also found him exceptionally irritating. Maybe the best way to reconcile these conflicting feelings was to get to know him better. Mibs nodded. "Yes, Jace, I would like to have dinner with you."

Aunt Bernie sighed loudly. "Well, it's about time! I was beginning to wonder if I was going to have to play matchmaker and set something up for you two myself." Bracing herself on the counter, she stood and reached for her walker. "I'm going to go to my room and lie down for a few minutes." She suggested, "Mibs, why don't you close up early today?" Then, turning to Jace, she added, "I hear they have a new chef at that fancy restaurant on the edge of town. If you come back in an hour, my niece would have time to freshen up."

Jace chuckled as Aunt Bernie walked away. Smiling at Mibs, he commented, "Your aunt is one interesting lady."

Chapter 16

Detective Trueblood leaned back, staring out the window in his office. His thoughts drifted to the night before and how Mibs' blue-green dress emphasized the red highlights of her hair. After leaving Monahan's following the Olsen incident, Jace returned to the police station and finished several items in his office before hurrying home to change. He tried on three different shirts before settling on a pale blue, linen, button-down style. He had surveyed his image in the mirror and berated himself. *Trueblood, you haven't been this nervous about a date since you asked Susie Evans to the homecoming dance.*

His breath caught when he stopped to pick Mibs up, and she opened the door. The dress was a perfect color for her complexion. It was a teal-colored, mid-length swing dress that Jace admired. Her hair was pinned up with wisps of curls framing her face, and her smile would have stopped most men in their tracks. He was sure that she had no idea how beautiful she was.

When they reached the restaurant, things went well. The food was delicious. Jace was pleased to find out that the slim, young woman enjoyed a dinner of meat and potatoes as much as he did.

"Mmm," Mibs murmured as she tasted the medium-well-done steak. "What Aunt Bernie heard about the new chef must be true. The asparagus in tarragon hollandaise sauce and the basil-garlic whipped potatoes are delicious; the steak is excellent."

"Mine is great, too," Jace agreed after swallowing his bite of orange ginger carrots. "Are you a good cook?"

Mibs raised an eyebrow and squinted at her date. "Do you ask all women you take to dinner that question? What about *you*? Are you a good cook?"

Stopping the fork just before the next bite reached his mouth, Jace glanced up in surprise. Setting the utensil aside, he tried not to laugh. "I wasn't trying to be chauvinistic. I don't assume all women spend their days in the kitchen. I like to cook and would like to learn how to do it better."

~~

"Oh, ahh, sorry," Mibs mumbled. *Awkward.* Pausing to quell her embarrassment, she said, "Yes, Jace, I do like to cook. I think it'd be fair to say that I can make some pretty decent meals."

Jace took a few more bites of food before he replied, "Then, maybe you could give me some lessons. How about baking? My grandmother made the best cinnamon rolls from scratch. I'd love to learn a recipe like that."

Mibs met his gaze and smiled. He smiled back. Soon they were both laughing.

"What else can we talk about?" she teased. "Let's try to find a subject where I won't stick my foot in my mouth again."

They soon discovered enough things in common that the conversation had flowed freely. Mibs shared memories from her high school days and others about her activities and classes at college. Jace told her about his more challenging cases while on the Nashville police force.

~~

Jace couldn't remember ever feeling such a

natural connection with any of the women he'd dated. There was a moment of disquietude when Mibs talked about singing in the choir at church, and Jace told her that he had quit going to church shortly after starting college. A brief flicker of sadness darted across her face before she changed the subject. They ended the meal by sharing a delectable piece of creamy, caramel-topped cheesecake.

When he walked her to the door that evening, Jace waited for Mibs to turn and look at him.

"I had an enjoyable evening." Mibs sighed.

"Yes. It was a great evening." Placing his hand on her shoulder, he smiled down at the charming girl. "I'd like to kiss you goodnight, but..." He raised a quizzical eyebrow waiting on her response.

"But, you're not automatically expecting to?" A hint of curiosity could be heard in Mibs' voice.

Touching his forehead to hers, he murmured, "Not expecting, just hoping."

Their first kiss was soft and gentle, but it affected them both. Jace seemed stunned for a second before he whispered, "You take my breath away."

~~

Jace was still daydreaming about the previous night when he realized that someone was talking to him. Pulling his attention back into the reality of the moment, he listened to Juan.

"Well? What do you think?" Juan Mendoza had been reviewing the information that Macey Buckmore had given them. "Buckmore's pictures gave us double the motives for James Hornsby."

"They certainly do that," Jace agreed. "However,

having an affair doesn't automatically make Hornsby the killer."

Macey Buckmore gave the detectives a report explaining how he had been hired by Jennifer Morris. Jennifer believed that her brother-in-law was cheating on her sister and had enlisted the private detective to follow James Hornsby. If she was right, she wanted proof to show her sister. Based on the folder Macey gave them, Ms. Morris had been correct.

Macey presented pictures of Hornsby going into a hotel with an attractive woman in her mid-thirties, pictures of him in a diner with the same woman, and of the couple sharing an intimate embrace in an underground parking lot.

"Greed and lust. Either one is a strong motive. But what we're missing is proof, especially since Hornsby has an alibi for the time of his wife's murder. The secretary insists that he was at work the morning that Jasmine Hornsby died. Maybe we should see if there's any reason that she could have been mistaken or if she may have lied to protect him."

"Yeah, and him being in his boss's office when the box of candy arrived seems a little too convenient."

"I agree, especially after hearing the receptionist describe how he lingered in the entranceway. He may have been watching for the delivery guy. Conway's assistant said that she was surprised when Hornsby hung around her desk and then asked about her grandchild. He could've been trying to make sure he was in his boss's office at just the right moment." Jace held up one of the pictures from Macey Buckmore. "Have we found out who the woman is yet?"

"No," Juan responded. "My first thought was that she was the secretary in Hornsby's office, a Maddi Dentin, but I confirmed that Dentin wasn't the woman in the pictures. So, I don't see why the secretary would lie about him being there. Do you have any thoughts on that?"

Jace stood up and pushed his chair back. "No, but let's talk to her again. Maybe Hornsby left without her noticing." Slipping his blazer back on, Jace followed the other detective out the door.

Twenty minutes later, Detectives Trueblood and Mendoza were sitting at a table in the Bernstein Electronic Company's employee break room.

Maddi Dentin waited, avoiding eye contact as she sat stiffly on the wooden chair across from them. "It's been a while now since the first time the police talked to me. I think my original statement would be the most accurate because my memory would've been fresher at that time." Ms. Dentin shook her head.

Detective Trueblood studied the woman for a moment. "Is there any way that Mr. Hornsby could have left without you noticing? Were you at your desk the whole day, or did you leave at any time? Perhaps for a break or lunch?"

"I did take two breaks, but neither was around the time you mentioned. I brought my lunch that day. I remember that because my friend, Sheryl from the inventory department, joined me at my desk, and we ate together between twelve-thirty and one o'clock."

"So, you didn't leave the area for any other reason between eleven-thirty and one o'clock?" he persisted.

Ms. Dentin let out a breath and leaned against the table. "I don't think so," she began and then suddenly stopped talking. "Wait! I *did* leave my desk that day. It would have been around eleven forty-five." Her mouth dropped open, and her eyes widened. "I went to the copy room and to the supply room."

"How long were you gone?" Trueblood asked.

"I would imagine that it was at least half an hour, maybe a little longer. I got back shortly before lunchtime. Mr. Hornsby wanted a hundred copies of a form printed, and he wanted them in a specific folder. He said that since the folder was a bright blue, it would be easier to keep track of it. That's why I went to the supply room; we don't keep that particular folder in the copy room. Making copies for the different accountants is such a common occurrence that it just blended into the day." A hint of unease entered the secretary's words as she added, "I didn't mean to leave that out. I really didn't! It just didn't come to mind."

"That's okay, Ms. Dentin. I'm glad you remembered and told us."

Jace stood and instructed Juan, "Let Ms. Dentin's boss know that she is going to be gone for a short time. Then, take her to the station to make an adjusted statement."

Turning, Jace shook her hand. "Thank y'all for talking to us. It shouldn't take too long for Detective Mendoza to drive you over for your statement. Is that all right with you, Ms. Dentin?"

"I...uhm...yes, of course," she stammered. "I'm not in any trouble for forgetting, am I?"

"Not at all. I appreciate your honesty." Jace gave her a reassuring smile before leaving the break room.

~~

Returning to the station, Detective Trueblood

knocked on Lieutenant Taylor's office door. "Do you have a minute, Hank?"

The lieutenant put down his pen, closed the folder of papers that he had been working on, and nodded. "Come in, Jace. What's on your mind?"

"It's the Hornsby and Morris deaths." Jace pulled back a chair and sat down across from his boss. "I'm pretty sure we know who the killer is." The detective gathered his thoughts before he continued, "We think it's the husband, James Hornsby. His alibi for each of the deaths seemed solid at first, but now they're shaky. My gut tells me he's guilty."

Lieutenant Taylor listened quietly to his detective, leaning back in his chair as the words sunk in. "Are you talking about both deaths? What about Murphy?"

"There isn't any evidence other than the typed card on Murphy. Even though he had a beef with Conway, he doesn't seem like the type of personality that would resort to murder. All bark, no bite," Jace said. "I've questioned and interviewed enough suspects to feel confident in saying that."

"Okay. Can we prove it? Anything other than questionable alibis?"

Jace sat back, crossing his arms across his chest. "No, and that's the problem. I need to find something to prove it. We have motives—money and another woman. We can show that he had the means. He had access to the candy that poisoned Jennifer Morris and the gun that killed her sister."

"I don't remember what the report said about the origin of the gun. Where did it come from?"

"According to Hornsby, the gun had been in a

locked box inside an antique sideboard. He ran across it one time when he was rummaging through the buffet. When he asked his wife about it, she explained that it had belonged to her father, who liked to target practice with friends when he was younger. After he died, she held on to it for sentimental reasons. Mr. Hornsby claimed that he had forgotten about it and didn't realize that it could still fire after all these years."

"I take it that you don't believe him?" Hank considered his detective's words.

"You're right about that. According to the forensic report, the revolver hadn't had a good cleaning in an exceptionally long time. However, it appears that someone had run a cleaning pad lightly through the barrel. Most of the patina had been wiped off the bullet that killed Jasmine Hornsby. A small box was found in the buffet containing a few old bullets that matched the one fired from the gun. Someone cleaned the weapon and bullet just enough so the gun wouldn't jam."

The lieutenant shook his head. "That's interesting. What about fingerprints? Were any found on the gun?"

"Oh, that's something, too. The only fingerprints on the gun were from Mrs. Hornsby. For an old gun that was quite likely used and handled by several people over the years, having only her fingerprints sends up a red flag." Jace slid the report across the desk. "And we have already established that it would be improbable that her crippled hands could have pulled the trigger on that heavy revolver."

"So, your theory is that James Hornsby shot his wife, then wrapped her hand around the gun before letting it drop to the floor," Taylor stated.

"That's what we think, but we can't prove it." Jace rubbed the back of his neck. "At least, we haven't proven it *yet*."

Chapter 17

Mibs heard the train's shrill whistle shortly before the guard gates began to descend. As the four o'clock express pulled to a stop in front of the newly remodeled station, she stepped onto the platform. In a few minutes, her best friend from college, Whitney Morgan, would be arriving for a weekend visit.

A conductor stepped off the train and placed a yellow footstool on the ground. The uniformed man greeted each passenger as they descended the steps, offering help as needed. A dozen people left the car before Mibs heard a familiar laugh.

Whitney stood smiling and joking with a young mother, two toddlers buzzing around the woman's legs.

After helping the children and their mom from the train, the conductor held out his hand toward Whitney. "May I help you with your bags, Miss?" the portly, gray-haired man asked.

"Well, you sure can!" The girl handed her sunflower yellow suitcase to him, and she looped a matching, long-strapped bag over her shoulder. Whitney stepped down, collected her suitcase, and gave him a little wave. "Thank you."

In return, she received a big smile and a tip of the hat from the courteous conductor.

"Whitney!" Mibs called as her friend made her way down the platform. The girls met with squeals and a big hug.

"It's so good to see you!" Mibs exclaimed.

Grinning from ear to ear, Whitney wrapped her

arm through her friend's. "I know what you mean, girl. It'll be great to catch up!" Whitney peppered Mibs with questions as they made their way to the car. "How's your aunt been since we last talked? I know you said that she was out of the wheelchair now. Have you made any new friends? Are the guys here cute?"

Mibs laughed. "Let's get your suitcase in the car and head home. Then, we can talk."

The two friends shared a pleasant ride as they chatted, and Mibs pointed out streets, houses, and businesses along the way. Because Havendale was much smaller than the big city that Whitney was used to, the tour didn't last long before they reached Monahan's Sewing Shop.

"Oh, wow, this is a cute building!"

"Come in and see the inside," Mibs invited. "Aunt Bernie's room is in the back. You'll be staying upstairs with me."

The bells jingled their usual greeting as the girls pushed the door open and entered the sewing shop. Aunt Bernie emerged from the back room. As soon as she saw Mibs with her friend, her aunt's face lit up with a wide smile. "At last! I get to meet the wonderful Whitney!" Aunt Bernie maneuvered her walker across the room.

Whitney laughed. "I don't know how wonderful I am, but it is so great to meet you, too!" The tall, friendly girl hurried toward Mibs' aunt. "Hello, Aunt Bernie. Is it okay if I call you Aunt Bernie? I feel like I already know you because of the many times Mibs has talked about you."

"Of course, you may. I wouldn't have it any other way. Now go; let Mibs show you her apartment upstairs. Then, when you've settled in, you can see how nicely she has arranged the sewing shop." With a shooing motion, the older lady directed them toward the back stairs.

Mibs' love for coordinating colors was evident throughout the cozy, efficiency apartment's living area. The warm brown shades of the furniture were accented with touches of yellow and maroon. The same color scheme was used with the curtains and throw rugs. A bathroom occupied a small area just past the kitchen. The galley kitchen was open to the living area, which consisted of a sofa, chair, and television centered on a sturdy bookcase. Behind the couch, a room divider partitioned off an alcove that housed a bed and dresser.

"Oh, I love this apartment!" Whitney exclaimed. "I feel like I could kick off my shoes, settle into this comfy couch, and just totally relax."

"Well, you make yourself as comfortable as you like," Mibs said. "This sofa folds out. You can have my bed, and I'll sleep here."

"Oh, no. I'm not taking your area," Whitney insisted. "I will sleep on the sofa. You know I usually stay awake later than you do anyway!" Whitney rolled her suitcase to a spot behind the couch. "Now, as for snacks..." The amiable, exuberant girl sauntered over to Mibs' old white refrigerator, cracking open the door as she asked over her shoulder, "Do you have any of that iced tea I like?" Straightening up, she smiled. "Oh! I should have known. You stocked up on my drink and favorite snacks. You even got Havarti cheese."

Before she could ask, Mibs opened a cupboard door and pointed to two boxes of sesame wheat crackers. "And I got your crackers, too. I thought we could make a run to the store for fruit and a good bottle of wine."

Clapping her hands, Whitney smiled. "Terrific!"

"That will be for snacking later," Mibs said. "Right now, let's go down so I can show you the shop. When we close at five, Aunt Bernie and I are taking you to the town's one and only Italian restaurant."

Whitney's sparkling voice filled the room as she perused the different areas of the shop. Mibs pointed out the sewing section, where she designed and sewed dresses and other clothing and where classes were conducted. The back wall held numerous notions and patterns. The front window showcased current fashions. But a significant part of the shop stocked materials: bolts of colorful cotton, brightly printed knits, linens, flannels, batiks, soft fleece, and even a few sheer silks.

"Oh, what beautiful fabric!" Whitney bubbled as she ran her hand over a silky, soft material. "It feels so smooth, and I love this peach color. Oh! This one is even better! I adore this purple shade."

Mibs couldn't help giggling. "I just knew you would like that. I was planning on making you an outfit for your birthday but wanted you to pick out the fabric. I love the feel of this, too. It isn't silk, but it has a blend of materials, rayon and viscose, that create a silk-like feel."

Whitney did a joyous little dance of excitement. "A custom-made outfit! You know me so well."

Grabbing her friend's hand, Mibs pulled her toward the back wall. "Come over and pick out a pattern, and then I'll take your measurements. That way, I'll have everything ready to start working on your *something new*. I'll probably change the pattern a bit. I usually like to start with a basic idea, then put in special touches that I think will harmonize with the wearer's style."

"What's all the laughing about back here?" Aunt Bernie's voice interrupted as she pushed her walker toward them.

"Aunt Bernie," Whitney said, "Mibs is going to make me a new outfit with the most scrumptious deep purple material." She held up three different patterns; one was for a sleeveless blouse and a pair of fitted slacks, the second one was a cropped bolero jacket and high-waisted skirt, and the third was for a color block midi dress. "I can't make up my mind. Which do you think would be best? Help me decide. Please!"

A few minutes later, having closed the sewing shop, Mibs, Whitney, and Aunt Bernie arrived at Alonzo's Ristorante and ordered their dinner. They all thought the sample platter sounded great. It featured small portions of three different kinds of pasta.

"I couldn't decide between lasagna, chicken alfredo, or eggplant parmesan," Mibs stated. "This sample dish is perfect. That way, I don't have to choose only one."

Bernie and Whitney both nodded.

"Definitely a perfect solution." Whitney gestured around the room. "This is a charming restaurant. I love the décor, especially the framed wine labels. And that mural on that wall! It evokes a feeling of being in the Italian countryside."

"It certainly does," Mibs answered.

While the trio waited for their entrees, they each enjoyed a glass of Chardonnay. "I'm glad that I'm not taking pain medicine anymore," Aunt Bernie said. "I missed my occasional glass of wine." Holding up her glass, she offered a toast. "To friendship and the blessing of having you two beautiful girls with me tonight."

"To friendship," Mibs toasted.

Clinking her wine glass lightly against Mibs', Whitney saluted, "Cheers!"

~~

The three women had a delightful time, laughing and chatting as they enjoyed their meals, blissfully unaware of the tall, dark-haired figure watching them from a barstool across the room. A scattering of ornamental palm trees partially hid him from the ladies' view, the plastic forest serving as a fence separating the bar from the main dining area. His vehement stare settled on Mibs for several minutes before it moved to her aunt. It remained there for only a moment before it moved to her friend, Whitney. His frown intensified as he recognized the former roommate.

"Interfering bitch," he mumbled through clenched teeth. "She's the one who's influencing Mibs."

Slamming his glass on the bar, he tossed several bills down. Ignoring the bartender's startled reaction, Nate stormed out of the restaurant.

Chapter 18

"Would you ladies like to see the dessert menu?" the rosy-cheeked waitress asked as she cleared away their dinner plates.

"Why don't you two have something?" Aunt Bernie said. "I don't think I can handle another bite."

As soon as Mibs glanced at her aunt, she could tell that the older woman was getting quite tired. "Aunt Bernie, we need to get you home."

"I am exhausted, but I don't want you and Whitney to cut your evening short." Aunt Bernie smiled. "Please order dessert. I've had their *Crème Brulee* before, and it's absolutely delicious."

"Actually," Whitney interrupted. "Mibs and I were going to get fruit, wine, and maybe rent a movie. You're closed tomorrow, so we'll probably just stay up late and visit."

"That's right. So why don't we head home?" Mibs suggested. "This meal was fabulous, but I'm ready to go to my apartment and relax."

After paying the bill along with a generous tip, the group made their way to the door. Moving slowly to accommodate Aunt Bernie's pace, they exited onto the sidewalk.

"Whitney, if you don't mind waiting with Aunt Bernie, I'll go get the car," Mibs proposed.

"Absolutely." Whitney wrapped her arms gently around the older woman's shoulders. "Maybe," she said, "while we're waiting, I'll get Aunt Bernie to tell me about something embarrassing you did when you were growing up."

Smiling back at her friend, she teased, "Well, now I don't know if I want to leave you two alone!" Mibs listened to her aunt's chuckle and Whitney's hearty laugh as she walked down the block to her parked car.

Mibs neared her car, slowing her pace as she dug into her purse for the ever-elusive keys. The whisper of footfalls made her stop. She glanced from side to side, but she saw no one. She even turned to scan the other side of the street. Shaking her head, she decided she must be hearing things. Climbing behind the wheel, checking her mirrors, and confirming the road behind her was just as empty as it had been ten seconds ago, she still had an uneasy feeling. *Is someone watching me?* Chasing the idea from her head, she started the car and drove around the block. She wanted to be on the right side when she picked up Aunt Bernie and Whitney, not wanting her aunt crossing the road in the dark. Two minutes later, she pulled up in front of the restaurant and grinned when she saw the two ladies with their heads together, talking as if Whitney had made good on her threat to worm childhood secrets out of Mibs' aunt.

They drove around to the back of the sewing shop to their usual parking spot. As they pulled to a stop, Whitney suggested that Mibs help Aunt Bernie into the building and get her settled inside.

"I noticed a grocery store we passed a few blocks back. If you don't mind me using your car, I'll run over and get the fruit and wine," Whitney offered.

"That would be great!" Mibs replied. "Don't worry about renting a movie tonight. I think we'll watch something we can stream online.

Mibs handed the car keys to her friend. Taking

the walker out of the vehicle and unfolding the metal legs, she placed it in front of her aunt. "Whitney, will you open the back door for us? The key is on the chain with the one for the car."

"Got it, girlfriend." She had the door unlocked and held it open by the time Aunt Bernie made her way to the entrance. Mibs stepped through the door after her aunt. Whitney waved. "I'll be back in a few minutes. Text if you think of anything special you want while I'm at the store."

~~

Cruising the isles of McDooley's Grocery Store, Whitney found a surprisingly extensive selection of fruit. Five minutes after scanning the enticing choices, Whitney decided on peaches, strawberries, blueberries, and crisp red apples. She stopped at the cheese section; creamy Brie and mild cheddar were added to the basket. Topping off the list was a semi-sweet local wine.

Just before reaching the checkout lane, she saw a display loaded with bunches of colorful mixed flowers. Thinking of Mibs' aunt, Whitney scooped up a cellophane-wrapped bouquet, adding it to the cart.

Ten minutes later, the girl popped open the trunk of Mibs' car. She had stacked the bag of groceries inside the compartment before picking up the bouquet. Deciding to keep the flowers up front, she started to shut the trunk.

A sudden pain shot through the side of her head. Dropping the bouquet and the keys, Whitney felt herself falling. As she hit the pavement of the parking lot, she felt more pain as blow after blow smashed down on her head, shoulders, and arms. Moments later, darkness took over.

Chapter 19

Tears slipped down Mibs' face. Feeling numb and helpless, she kept vigil outside the ICU at Havendale Community Hospital.

~~

Jace paced up and down the hall as he listened to the voice on his cell phone. Mendoza leaned against the stark white hospital wall with his arms folded across his chest. Ending the call, Jace sat down next to Mibs.

Gently touching her hand, he said, "They're taking good care of her. The ambulance got her here quickly, and there was a team waiting when they pulled up to the emergency entrance doors."

Mibs slowly nodded. "I know. But why is it taking so long? Why hasn't anyone talked to us yet and told us how she's doing?"

"They had to take X-rays and run tests. That all takes time."

Rummaging through her purse, Mibs pulled out a tissue and wiped her tears. "Why would anyone do this? If it was a robbery, why didn't they just take her purse? It was sitting in plain sight in the grocery cart. Why did they have to hurt her?"

One of the officers, Maxine Schroeder, had checked the registration in the glove compartment after Whitney had been loaded into an ambulance. Schroeder recognized the name of the car's owner, Mirabelle Monahan. She had met the young woman during the murder investigation of Jennifer Morris, and Schroeder speculated that Trueblood would want to be notified. She made the call, both as a courtesy to a senior officer and because it seemed like the most efficient way to get information. The driver's license found at the scene showed Whitney Morgan was from a town 300 miles away. A friend or a relative close by would be a quicker contact. Jace went over and told Mibs that Whitney had been beaten and taken to the hospital. Upset and worried at the news, Mibs accepted his offer to drive her to Havendale General.

Releasing a long breath, Jace hesitated. "We're considering it more of a deliberate attack than an attempted robbery."

"What do you mean?" Mibs shook her head in disbelief.

"An elderly couple told the officers that a man walked up behind Whitney and hit her with something that appeared to be a baseball bat." Lightly placing a supportive hand on her arm, he added, "We don't know for sure, but we think it may have been Olsen. The height, hair color, and approximate age fit his description. I have a detective taking a copy of Olsen's picture to show the witnesses; hopefully, they can give us an ID from the photo. The couple reported hearing him yell something like, 'You shouldn't have gotten between us.'"

Mibs' complexion paled as she moaned, "Oh, no! Then, it's my fault."

"No. This isn't your fault. Whether it was Olsen or someone else, the attacker is the one responsible," Jace reassured her. "We've already sent out an order to bring him in. Even though we don't have proof yet, we can still pull him in as a person of interest."

Before Jace could say more, a tall, stoop-shouldered man wearing a white lab coat approached. "Are you Miss Monahan?" the gentle-voiced physician inquired.

Mibs froze in place. "Yes."

"I'm Doctor Manning. I talked to Miss Morgan's parents on the phone. They said that they would be here in a few hours. They also said to add you to the list of contacts and try to answer any questions you may have."

Tears filled her eyes again. "How is Whitney? Will she be all right?"

Taking the chair on the other side of Mibs, the doctor gave a weary nod. "I believe she will recover. However, we want to keep an eye on her for the next forty-eight hours. She sustained hard blows to the head. It caused a concussion, and she was unconscious for a while. Miss Morgan is awake now, but we've given her some heavy pain medicine because of all her injuries."

"What other injuries does she have, Doctor?" Mibs' voice cracked.

"Our exam shows that she was hit at least five times. Besides the concussion, she sustained a broken arm, numerous deep bruises, and some lacerations." In a more cheerful tone, he said, "Fortunately, she doesn't seem to have any internal injuries or bleeding. It will take some time, but barring any unforeseen circumstances, she should make a full recovery." Shifting his gaze from Mibs to Detective Trueblood, then back to the shaken girl, he asked, "Is there anything else you want to know?"

"Can I see her?"

"You can go in, but she won't be aware of her surroundings because of the narcotics," Doctor Manning answered.

"Doctor Manning, I'm Detective Sergeant Trueblood. I'm on the Havendale Police Force. Will we be able to ask Miss Morgan questions about her attack tonight?"

"Not at this time." Doctor Manning shook his head. "I would suggest that you wait until tomorrow afternoon."

Mibs reached for Jace's hand. "I would like Detective Trueblood to come in with me as a friend," she entreated.

~~

A few minutes later, Mibs stood next to the hospital bed, sadly watching her friend. Whitney's dark, curly hair cascaded across the pillow and made the bandage wrapped around her head appear even more noticeable. Her right arm was encased in a stiff cast. An IV needle was taped to the back of her other hand, and liquid slowly dripped into the attached tube as a rhythm of beeps and whirls reverberated from the monitors.

Mibs picked up her friend's hand and gave it a light squeeze. "Whitney, I'm so sorry," she whispered.

The injured woman's eyes opened, and a soft smile parted her lips. "What are you sorry about? Did you drink too much wine, too?"

"Wine?" Mibs questioned. "I don't understand."

Jace touched Mibs' shoulder. "The doctor said she wasn't likely to know what was going on. See, she's already sleeping again." He pulled a chair close to the side of Whitney's hospital bed. "Sit down. I would tell you to go home and rest, but I know you want to stay. I'll go get you a cup of coffee; then I'm going to see if any of our officers have found more information about what happened. Detective Mendoza will be right outside

143

the door. If you want to take a break or need anything, let him know."

~~

After returning with a large coffee, Jace set it on a nearby ledge and watched Mibs for a moment. She sat, focused on Whitney. Tears brimmed her eyes, and a heartsick expression was on her face. Jace wished that he could take the physical pain from Mibs' friend and the mental anguish from her, but the best he could do was to find the deranged man who had done this.

Stepping out of the room, Jace nodded to Detective Mendoza. "Juan, I'll send someone over to relieve you. When he or she gets here, go home and get some rest. I'd like you back here first thing in the morning. I've already discussed with Miss Monahan the importance of caution while Olsen is still running around free. She agreed when I told her I wanted to request security for her and Miss Morgan. For now, I don't want either of these ladies left unguarded. We don't want to take a chance if this guy tries something else."

"No problem, Jace. I'll make sure whoever takes my place understands that, and I'll be here early."

"Thanks. I'll have someone come over to replace you before noon tomorrow. See you at the station after that. And if Miss Monahan wants to leave, call me. I'll come over or send an officer. I don't want her going out by herself."

"Don't worry. Go do what you have to do," Mendoza urged.

Chapter 20

Jace stood before a large whiteboard stretched along one wall in the police station. A timeline was drawn across the top with notes written under each date. Below that were numerous pictures and more information, including numbers, names, and lists of physical evidence.

Sergeant Brice Long and Detective Juan Mendoza sat at nearby desks as Lieutenant Hank Taylor watched from a spot near the cluttered bank of computer monitors. Several patrol officers called in to help with the cases moved closer to the crime board.

Jace faced his fellow officers and inquired, "Before we review the information on the Morris/Hornsby cases, do we have any leads on Nate Olsen or the attack on Miss Morgan?"

Sergeant Long shook his head. "Not yet. Olsen seems to have dropped off the face of the earth."

"Did we contact the police in his hometown and have them talk to his family?" Lieutenant Taylor asked. "Do we know what kind of vehicle he owns? If he rented a car from a local dealership? Or if he may be using a relative or friend's vehicle?"

"We have an APB out on the description of the car and license listed with the DMV," Sergeant Long answered. "Before he lived on the college campus, his home address was in Bellcrest. We've been in contact with the local police there, and they'll let us know if there's anything new to share."

Lieutenant Taylor responded, "Good. Keep me in the loop if anything comes up." Turning to Jace, he added, "Continue the security on Miss Morgan and Miss Monahan for now. I have a feeling that Olsen hasn't gone far."

Jace nodded, turning back to the crime board. "I think everyone is up-to-date on the evidence we've compiled so far on the Morris/Hornsby deaths, but let's do a quick review and see if anything significant stands out." Grabbing a narrow yardstick, the detective used it to point to a picture of Conway, vice-president of the Bernstein Electronics Company. "We no longer believe that Conway was the target for the poisoned candy. However, we haven't made that public knowledge. We don't want the killer to know that we are concentrating our search away from Bernstein Electronics and toward someone who may have wanted Jennifer Morris dead." Jace stepped to the middle of the board and indicated the picture of Ms. Morris; then he pointed to Jasmine Hornsby's image. "Who wanted both Jennifer Morris and her sister Jasmine Hornsby dead?"

Detective Mendoza spoke up. "The logical suspect would be Hornsby's husband."

"Yeah, but doesn't he have alibis for the time of each of the deaths?" Sergeant Long frowned.

"We thought that he had, but now they're a bit shaky."

"Hmm? How so? I hadn't heard," said Brice.

"We talked to his secretary at work," Detective Trueblood answered. "She remembered that she'd been away from her desk for at least half an hour. The timeline would've been close, but if he hurried, Hornsby could have driven to his house and back within twenty minutes. That would leave him ten minutes to kill his wife."

Detective Delgado, a young man with a swarthy complexion and intense eyes, interrupted. "Ten minutes doesn't seem like enough time to shoot someone, stage the crime scene, and leave without anyone seeing something. And you would have to be sure that you didn't run into any traffic problems on the way there and back."

"That's a good point, Delgado, but if you think about it, there's sufficient time, as long as you have everything ready and know no one other than the victim will be home." Trueblood leaned against a desk and folded his arms across his chest. "Let's figure that there were no problems with the drive. If there had been, Hornsby would've either hoped that no one missed him, or he'd make up an excuse to explain his absence." Detective Trueblood ran his fingers through his hair. "The housekeeper, Jane de Bois, went to the store every week at the same time, so Hornsby knew his wife would be alone. According to the housekeeper, she helped Jasmine Hornsby use the chair lift to get upstairs and then aided her into a wheelchair. Mrs. Hornsby wanted to spend some time in the room where they kept the doll collection. That's the room where they found her body. Jasmine Hornsby was frail, and her illness limited her ability to move quickly. She wouldn't be expecting her husband to attack her. Even if she did see him aim the gun at her, she wouldn't have been able to run or fight him off."

Trueblood straightened and considered his team. "I could be wrong, so I don't want us to stop pursuing other avenues, but we should be following up all leads and tips. There is nothing to indicate that the only other relative, a cousin, had anything to do with the deaths. And, because of a lack of evidence, we've released the salesman we previously brought in on suspicion. They are both being kept under surveillance just in case we missed something. Call it a gut feeling, but I believe that James Hornsby killed both his wife and his sister-in-law."

Juan Mendoza passed several pictures to the other detectives. "I think most of you know the local PI, Macey Buckmore."

A moan and a few chuckles could be heard from the assembled group when the well-known, colorful character was mentioned.

"He gave us these pictures. You can see the guy in the photos is Hornsby. We recently IDed the woman as Wendy Black, a local physical therapist. To be precise, she was Mrs. Hornsby's PT. She'd go by the Hornsby home twice a week to help Jasmine with mobility exercises."

Moving up to stand next to Trueblood, Mendoza continued. "Apparently, Black and the husband started having an affair several months ago. There is enough motive to implicate him as a likely suspect between the wife's multimillion-dollar bank account and the 'other' woman."

Jace said, "We can connect James Hornsby with both the poisoned candy and the gun. According to his own statement, he knew about the gun, and he knew where it was kept. As far as his sister-in-law's poisoning, it seemed almost too convenient that he happened to be in the right place to be given the box of candy to take home." Trueblood took a deep breath. "So, he also had means and opportunity."

"Okay, Sergeant," Lieutenant Taylor interrupted. "Now, give me some proof, so we can get an arrest warrant from the DA."

Jace nodded. "Brice, bring the physical therapist, Black, in for questioning. Don't let her know what we suspect yet. Tell her that we're questioning everyone who'd been in the Hornsby house recently, hoping that maybe they saw something significant without realizing it. Make it sound like we're asking for help."

"Will do," replied Sergeant Long. "Maybe she'll let something slip that we can use."

Jace shrugged. "Maybe she knows something, or maybe she doesn't have anything to do with the murders. Try to get an idea of how she really feels about James Hornsby."

"Got it." Brice grabbed his jacket. "I'll take Delgado with me. He's been wanting to get out in the field more."

"Sounds like a good idea," Jace agreed, then tapped a closed fist on Mendoza's shoulder. "Even though we've run through the evidence more than once, let's do it again. Bring everything to my office: paperwork, physical evidence, witness statements, anything and everything relevant to these murders."

Detective Trueblood turned to the others. "The rest of y'all get on computers and phones. We need to start checking traffic cameras along the route between Hornsby's work and his home on the day of his wife's murder. See if he shows up in any of them. Bernstein Electronics only has security cameras on the front entrances of their building. Hornsby could have used any of several unmonitored exits from the back area to leave that day. Also, check his personal finances. Does he have any significant debts? Any gambling problems? Any large, unexplained withdrawals or deposits?"

Tayler spoke up. "Share anything you find and

make sure it's added to the crime board."

"Juan," Jace addressed Mendoza as they walked to his office. "How was Ms. Morgan doing today when you took your shift at the hospital?"

"Doing much better. It's going to take some time for all the bruises and abrasions to heal, but the concussion shouldn't cause any permanent problems, according to the doctor's report." They reached the office with Detective Trueblood's name on it and stepped through the doorway. "The hospital said they were releasing her tomorrow, and her parents will drive her back home."

"Good, she will probably be safer away from here," Jace stated. "Make sure there's police protection until she's in her parents' car and heading out of town."

"I was planning on relieving the officer at the hospital in the morning and staying until Whitney leaves," Juan quickly announced.

"It's Whitney now? You were calling her Ms. Morgan yesterday." Jace raised a brow at the younger detective, a hint of a smile spreading across Juan's features. "You seem to have taken a personal interest in this lady."

"Ah..." Juan stammered for a moment before he grinned and shrugged. "We have had a good bit of time to talk while I was taking my turn on security duty." His eyes seemed to spark as he talked about Mibs' friend. "She's a fascinating and fun-loving person."

Jace chuckled as he sat down in the chair behind his desk. "Well, after you see Ms. Morgan into her car tomorrow, head back here. I want to finish up our review, then, either tomorrow or Thursday, we should go back to the Hornsby house one more time. I can't help but feel like we missed something." Trueblood tapped his pencil on the desk as he thought about the case. "But for now, Juan, run down to the evidence lockup and bring the items from the crime scene. Get one of the clerks to help you. I meant it when I said we're going through everything again," he emphasized, settling into the chair, anticipating a long day ahead.

Chapter 21

Jace and Juan were still combing through evidence long after most of the other detectives had headed out for dinner and, hopefully, some well-deserved sleep. Jace had tried to get Juan to leave when he realized the time and remembered that the other detective had started his day at six that morning.

Juan refused to go until they had searched through all the boxes of physical evidence that had been stacked across Detective Trueblood's desk and floor. While going through the containers, Jace pulled out the clear evidence bag, which held a small, blue piece of thread. Recalling what Lieutenant Taylor had said about the possible way that the door might have been locked from outside the room made him remember that it was Mibs Monahan who first called his attention to the thread snagged on the old-fashioned lock. "It could be evidence," she had said with a determination. Now, Jace was sure that the feisty redhead had been right about the 'thread of evidence.'

The pair finally called it a day and walked out of the police station a little after nine o'clock. After getting home and taking a quick shower, Jace heated up leftovers and sat down in a worn but comfortable recliner situated in his current bedroom. The small space on the first floor of the sprawling Georgian Colonial he'd inherited was the most accessible room to remodel. Some rewiring and a good coat of paint at least made this sleeping area livable. He planned to eventually make the spacious room at the top of the stairs into the master suite, but for now, he had stuffed his bed, dresser, TV, and recliner into this room. A couple of pictures cut the bareness of the walls, while the majority of his personal items were still secured in a storage locker across town.

Even though he was a reasonably good cook, Jace was leery about using the old stove and appliances that his Uncle Ezekiel had left. For now, his diet mainly consisted of take-out and microwavable foods. It wasn't the healthiest choice, but hopefully, there would be enough time in his busy schedule to quickly get the kitchen redone. Jace hadn't been able to start pulling out cabinets and getting the old appliances hauled away yet. He hadn't planned on the added job of emptying the unbelievable amount of dishware in the overstuffed cupboards and mountain of cookware, cleaning products, and outdated canned goods in the pantry. He was still working on that chore, hoping to have everything cleared out in a few days.

The roof and the foundation were the first things he'd had checked when he inherited the house. Although the roof needed the shingles replaced, it was basically sound. The boards used to build this expansive, symmetrical house were thick, solid timbers. Jace hired a five-star-reviewed basement specialist to seal some minor leaks and shore up one of the walls that had shifted slightly over the past decades. The roof and basement work had been completed before he moved in. Knowing that rain wouldn't be dripping on him or the foundation moving underneath, Jace was ready to tackle most of the remodeling on his own. If he ran into anything beyond his ability, he wouldn't hesitate to ask for help or hire a professional. Although Jace had a good understanding of electrical circuitry, the cautious side of him decided to hire an electrician. If the place only needed a few new plugs or a couple light fixtures changed, he would have taken care of it. However, the whole house needed updated wiring, as well as a new circuit box. Jace knew his limits.

A lot of the desired remodeling he could do himself. Jace had learned a great deal about carpentry and home building from his father, Christopher Trueblood. For many years, Chris Trueblood was one of the most sought-after contractors in the Nashville area. Jace had worked with his father during summer breaks from the time he was fifteen until his last year in college. Choosing a career in law enforcement instead of following in his father's footsteps had surprised his parents. They suspected that his decision was based on circumstances surrounding his younger brother Conner's death and the fact that the killer was never brought to justice.

At the age of seventeen, Conner was killed in what the police had called a random robbery. Several other people in the area had reported being hit over the head while using an ATM machine. They were either stunned or completely knocked out. When each victim's head cleared enough to call for help, he or she realized that the cash they had just withdrawn was gone. The blow to Conner's temple did more than immobilize him for a few minutes. It killed him.

Connor and Jace had been close. Jace, nineteen and in college at the time, never got over the loss of his brother. He switched his planned major from business to law enforcement and became a police officer soon after graduation. Despite his career choice, Jace was knowledgeable about home repairs. Even though his parents moved to Arizona after retirement, his father was still more than willing to answer any questions Jace had while reworking the old house.

With his new job in Havendale, Jace wouldn't be able to take time off to fly out to Arizona and visit his folks. He missed his mom and dad. They talked on the phone at least every two weeks. More often, if Jace had a remodeling problem. The calls were helpful, but they weren't the same as seeing them in person. He missed the pat on the shoulder from Dad and the kiss on the cheek from Mom. He wished that he had his father's skilled hands to help him with the work on this old house, and one of his mother's home-cooked meals would be great, too. Jace sighed as he pondered the picture hanging on the wall.

Gazing at the old family photo usually caused two conflicting feelings to sweep across his thoughts. A sense of pride engulfed him as he focused on his parents sitting on a rough-hewn rocker bench; his brother Conner and he were standing behind, shoulder to shoulder. Then a feeling of sadness took over as Jace dwelt on the fact that he would never see his brother again. Taking a deep breath, he shook the thoughts away and finished the leftover chicken alfredo he'd warmed in the microwave.

He knew that he should go to bed soon and rest up for the busy day tomorrow but realized that sleep wouldn't find him for a while. Too keyed-up. Too much on his mind. He headed back into the kitchen, rinsed his dish, and set it in the sink. Grabbing a collapsed cardboard box, Jace unfolded it and taped the seams. Setting it on the floor in front of the counter, he began filling it with storage containers, plastic cups, and several kitchen utensils that he couldn't identify. When it was full, he taped it shut, labeled it with a black marker, and started on the next box.

Chapter 22

As soon as Mibs stepped out of the elevator on the third floor of the hospital, she caught the sound of Whitney's bubbly laugh coming from down the hall. By the time she reached the door, she had heard a deep voice responding to her friend. Entering the room, Mibs smiled when she saw Whitney sitting on the edge of the bed, waiting to be discharged. She was dressed in a bright pink t-shirt and a pair of vintage overalls with flower patches embroidered across the bib. A smaller bandage had replaced the previous, large one on her head. The cast on her arm was already partially covered with signatures.

Detective Mendoza was perched on the edge of a chair, leaning toward Whitney as they talked and laughed. Her smile drew attention away from the discolored bruising along her face. Mibs hesitated to interrupt the pair, who seemed to be enjoying each other's company and thought about stepping back out of the room for a few minutes. Before she could do so, Detective Mendoza turned around and halfway rose from the chair. His features switched from an air of leisure to one of instant preparedness. But as soon as he met Mibs' gaze, he relaxed again.

Once standing, he indicated the now-empty chair. "Miss Monahan, please sit here."

The detective moved past her and headed toward the door, back in a professional mode.

"Thank you, Detective Mendoza," Mibs called to him.

"Yes, thank you, Juan." Whitney raised one eyebrow as she smiled.

After stopping to nod at Mibs and wink at Whitney, he strode through the doorway. "I'll be outside if you need anything."

Giggling and taking both Whitney's hands in hers, Mibs tilted her head. "You seem to have made a friend – quite a handsome friend." Giving the girl a crooked smile, Mibs shook her head in amazement. "Whitney, only you could find a cute guy while stuck in a hospital room."

"It's good to meet a nice guy." Whitney put on an innocent expression before turning serious. "It's especially good to know all men are not like the Neanderthal that's stalking you."

Mibs sighed. "I'm so sorry, Whitney, that you were hurt because of me."

"I wasn't hurt because of you. I was hurt because that creep is crazy! If he hadn't fixated on you, it would have been on someone else."

"But I feel responsible." Her stomach clenched.

"Hey, let's think of the bright side. I got to lay around in a bed for a couple days, getting waited on and pampered. When I get home, my mother is going to be hovering and spoiling me. She will probably buy unnecessary presents." Whitney paused and tapped her chin. "Hmm, maybe I should give her a hint about this bag I saw. It's the cutest butterscotch clutch with a gold-colored latch."

"Oh, Whitney!" Threatening tears were chased away with the need to laugh. "I love that you are such a positive person!"

Her friend shrugged. "And I met a 'teddy bear' of a police detective." Leaning forward, Whitney whispered, "We exchanged phone numbers. He's going to call me when I get home."

"Well, that will be a long-distance relationship."

Whitney took a drink of water before she responded. "Mibs, I don't think I'm ready to get serious about any guy yet. But I'll enjoy spending time talking to an interesting person like Juan. If we do decide to pursue more than just a casual friendship, I don't think the miles apart will matter." Taking another sip from her cup, she shrugged. "And it would give me another reason besides you to come back and visit Havendale."

Their conversation was interrupted when Whitney's parents arrived. Mrs. Morgan was an older version of Whitney. As she entered, the scent of floral perfume filled the air. A chiffon dress accented her full but shapely figure with coordinating shoes and purse, mirroring her daughter's love for clothing and accessories. Their similarities also included the ever-present, bubbly personality.

"Whitney, my baby, are you ready to go home?" Jeanette Morgan engulfed her daughter in a careful embrace. "I'm worried that you may get tired before we get all the way home. Your father and I thought that we could drive for a couple hours, then stop at a hotel to let you rest."

Clasping her mother gently on the back, Whitney moved the worried parent lightly away. "I think that I'll be fine, Mom. I don't see why we can't go home today. I'll rest better in my own room."

"Well...we'll see." Mrs. Morgan turned to her husband. "What do you think, Sugar?"

As he ambled forward, Mr. Morgan, dressed in comfortable brown slacks and tan pull-over shirt, appeared laid-back. "I think we'll see how the ride goes. We can make frequent stops, and if Whitney needs to rest, she can let us know."

Placing her hand on Jeanette Morgan's arm, Mibs implored, "Please, call me and let me know how Whitney is doing. I won't be able to rest unless I know she's recovering well."

Whitney reached over and took her mother's other arm. "Mom, tell Mibs that this isn't her fault. She's feeling needlessly guilty."

"Oh, baby!" Jeannette turned and threw her arms around Mibs, giving her a motherly hug. "Don't you go blaming yourself for what happened. You're a sweet girl. You didn't cause this."

"That's right, Mibs." Stepping closer, Mr. Morgan crossed his arms. His dark skin couldn't hide the flush of anger highlighting his features. "We're going to take Whitney home and keep an eye on her, probably more than she wants us to. In the meantime, I hope this vile man won't bother you again."

"I'll be fine," Mibs mumbled. "I'm sure I'll be fine."

Mr. Morgan shook his head. "Miss Monahan...Mibs, I'm financially able to hire a bodyguard or a private detective or both. Why don't I arrange something to ensure your safety?"

"I don't think that will be necessary." Mibs smiled. "The police have been keeping a close eye on me and my home."

"Well, okay, but let me know if you change your mind."

Stepping up to Detective Mendoza, who stalwartly stood guard in the doorway, Mr. Morgan questioned him in a calm but authoritative voice. "What about this guy who attacked my daughter? Why haven't the police apprehended him yet? I would think that finding him would be a priority."

Juan looked Leroy Morgan in the eyes. "The entire Havendale Police Force is taking this case very seriously. We haven't found the attacker yet, but he can't stay hidden forever. Since the couple who saw the attack identified Nate Olsen's photo, we were able to distribute his picture to our police force. Believe me, there's a lot of effort being put forth to catch this man. In the meantime, both Miss Morgan and Miss Monahan have had an officer watching out for their safety." Glancing over at Whitney, the detective said, "I won't leave your daughter's side until I see her pulling away in the car with you and your wife."

"Humph. Let me know as soon as he is arrested. And...let us know when he goes to trial!"

A wheelchair was pushed into the room, and an attendant brought in discharge papers to be signed. A short time later, Whitney was sitting in the back seat of her father's car and waving at Mibs as the silver Lincoln sedan pulled away from the curb.

When Mibs turned around, Detective Mendoza was standing behind her on the sidewalk.

"Where do you want to go, Miss Monahan?"

Mibs smiled at the detective. "Are you my escort now?"

"No, not me. Jameson, the same officer who brought you here, is waiting at the edge of the parking lot. I'll walk you to his squad car. Then, I've got to get back to the station." Juan hesitated with a dubious expression on his face. "Because of budget restraints, our lieutenant was informed that we could only keep the round-the-clock police security for another day. Neither Trueblood nor I am happy with that, but it isn't our call. By the

161

way, Trueblood left orders at the station to notify him if anything occurs concerning you or Monahan's Sewing Shop, no matter what time of day or night."

Mibs squared her chin and reassured the detective. "It's okay. I know help will only be a call away, and I'll be careful and extra alert if I go anywhere."

"Please, do that, Miss Monahan."

She called to mind the offer that Whitney's father had made but decided that she wouldn't let Olsen intimidate her into hiding. She was now more furious than afraid. "I will. Thank you, Detective." She turned toward the parked cruiser. "I better get back to my sewing shop. I have things to work on, too." As they approached the police car that would drive her home, Mibs stopped and looked up at the dark-haired officer beside her. "Juan, be good to Whitney. She's a wonderful person and a good friend."

"She *is*. I hope she'll become my friend, too."

Nodding, Mibs walked toward the door that Officer Jameson held open for her, turned back, and smiled. "Juan, please tell Detective Trueblood thanks for taking care of Whitney, my aunt, and me."

Juan returned the smile and gave a short salute before turning around, quick steps taking him back toward his vehicle.

Chapter 23

Mibs returned to the building that served as both a business and a home for her and Aunt Bernie. Shortly after, she left again – this time with Aunt Bernie – pulling her car out of the small parking lot behind the shop. She quickly spotted Officer Jameson's cruiser, which followed her and her aunt down Main Street. The Monahan women were heading back toward the medical complex in Havendale. Driving half a block past the hospital, Mibs stopped in front of the orthopedic specialists' offices. Aunt Bernie had been moving with just the support of her cane when she was in her own mini-apartment and in the shop when she didn't think Mibs was watching. Mibs had noticed but hadn't said anything.

After taking the walker out of the back seat, Mibs set it up by the car's opened front door. Aunt Bernie motioned for her to move her offered arm away and pulled herself out of the vehicle. Grabbing the walker and turning toward the building's entrance, she stopped and smiled at Mibs.

"Bring the cane too, please. I plan on using it on the way out."

Amused, Mibs nodded. "I had a feeling you would say that."

Forty-five minutes later, they were heading back home. The walker was folded and resting in the back. The cane was clutched in Aunt Bernie's hands in the front seat.

"Remember, the doctor okayed you using just the

cane as needed, but he told you not to overdo things. You are not ready to run any races," Mibs cautioned.

"I know, my dear. Slow and steady is the way to go."

When they returned to the sewing shop, Mibs waved at Officer Jameson as she pulled around back, and he parked across the street.

After insisting that her aunt rest for a few minutes following her trip to the doctor's office, Mibs headed to the front of the sewing shop to remove the 'Closed' sign, turning on lights as she went. She had no sooner reached the front door when the back door buzzer sounded. Hurrying to the delivery area in the rear of the building, she peeked through the small glass window in the middle of the door. Mibs smothered a moan when she realized the delivery truck driver was over an hour early. She had hoped there would be time to finish up some mending before the bolts of new material arrived. "Oh, well," she muttered. "I may as well get the order checked in and put away now instead of later."

Occasionally, someone new would bring the order to Monahan's, but today it was the usual driver. "Hello, Willy," Mibs greeted the middle-aged man.

Willy had a melancholy appearance accentuated by his downturned mustache and dark, brooding eyes. His features belied his personality as a good-hearted, friendly fellow.

Although he seldom mentioned it, Mibs knew that he had been in the military with a Special Forces unit. She suspected that the faraway, sad expression he sometimes got resulted from seeing too much violence during his thirty years in the service.   Willy usually accepted the cup of coffee and sweet roll that Aunt Bernie always had ready when they knew that a delivery was due at the shop.

Standing at Willy's heel was a mahogany-colored dog named Shadow.   She had chocolate-colored eyes, black ears, and a black mask around her mouth. Despite the sturdy build, the dog had an elegant appearance.   Shadow was an appropriate name for her since she stayed close to Willy's leg, moving when he moved, stopping when he stopped and keeping a constant, loving eye on her human companion. Shadow had been overseas with Willy before his retirement.   The six-year-old Belgian Malinois and the retired sailor were both veterans and had a special bond.

"Afternoon, missy." The driver handed over the invoice for the ordered items. "I see there's a large order today."

"Yes, I sold a lot of my inventory during the holiday sales." Mibs stepped outside, followed him to the back of the delivery truck, and waited as he unlocked the door.   Mibs noticed that Officer Jameson's car had moved closer to check the delivery truck.

Willy rolled the door up and stepped into the back. Shadow jumped in, too, and watched as her master began moving cargo.   After sliding numerous boxes closer to the entrance, he stepped down and passed several smaller items to Mibs.

"If you take those in, I'll start loading these larger containers onto the dolly." Reaching into the back corner of the truck, Willy pulled down the utility cart and started stacking boxes on it.

"Do you want to come with me, Shadow?" Mibs rubbed the dog's ears.

Shadow wagged her tail but checked with Willy before moving.

"Go on, Shadow," he told his canine friend. "We both know those Monahan ladies keep dog biscuits on hand, especially for you." Pointing to the door and saying okay, Willy signaled the dog.

The dog hurried through the door, making her way from the storage room to the small counter where Mibs and Bernie made coffee and tea and where they kept a glass mason jar filled with treats for their four-legged visitor. Before Mibs could reach the snack area, Aunt Bernie had met up with Shadow and was pulling out several biscuits.

"Aunt Bernie, I thought you were resting."

She bent down and handed the treats to the dog. "I heard the back door and figured it was Willy, so I had to come out and say hello to this beautiful girl." She gently rubbed Shadow's head. "Isn't that right, sweet lady?"

The order was brought in and confirmed against the invoice. Willy handed over a travel mug and asked for his coffee to go. "I have a really tight schedule today, so I can't linger." After a quick wave, the driver climbed into his truck's cab and nodded at Mibs as he started the truck. Shadow, hanging out the window, barked goodbye as they pulled away.

Chapter 24

Mibs loaded a cart with some of the new items and pushed them to the display area. She opened a box of notions and had just started to hang packs of elastic on a pegboard when the phone rang. At the same time, three women entered the store.

"Hello, ladies. Please wander around while I answer the phone. I'll be with you shortly."

As the customers walked toward a rack holding bolts of calico cotton, Mibs rushed to the counter and picked up the phone lying by the cash register.

"Monahan's Sewing Shop, how may I help you?"

"Miss Monahan?"

"Yes, what can I do for you?"

"This is Janie de Bois. Do you remember me, the housekeeper for the Hornsbys' home?"

"Yes, of course, Janie. How are you doing?"

"Oh, I'm holding up, I guess. I haven't decided what to do yet. My nephew wants me to move and buy a little place near him. I'm thinking about it, but I've lived in Havendale for over twenty years now, and I have a lot of friends here."

"Are you still at the Hornsby house?" Mibs had picked up a pencil and was doodling on a pad by the phone. "Does Mr. Hornsby want you to stay on as his housekeeper?'

"He did ask me to stay until the estate is settled. I get the impression that he wants the property sold as soon as possible. Even if he decides to live here, I don't think I could stay. Jasmine and Jennifer were very dear to me. There are too many memories here."

"Is there anything I can do to help, Janie?"

"Well, that's why I called." It sounded like the woman sucked in a breath. "The law firm in charge of Jasmine's and Jennifer's estates wants me to go through the sisters' doll collection with their local representative, John Marshal. He's bringing a woman from the museum with him." Janie hesitated. "It's hard for me to even go into that room now. After the police released the area, I had to hire a cleaning crew to come in and take care of the bloodstains. When the dolls are removed, I'm going to see if Mr. Hornsby will let me hire a contractor to replace the flooring and repaint the walls." The quiver in Janie's voice had turned to low sobs.

"Oh, Janie, I can't imagine how hard this has been for you," Mibs sympathized, then remained silent for a few moments hoping to give the housekeeper a chance to regain her composure.

After clearing her throat and taking a couple of deeper breaths, Janie continued. "Sorry about that, Miss Monahan. I didn't mean to get so emotional."

"Don't apologize. It is an emotional situation," Mibs assured her. "What is it that you would like me to do?"

"I know that Jasmine showed you the entire collection, and you talked about touching up any that needed repairs. I was wondering if you had finished or even started with what she wanted to have done. And...well, and I was hoping you would help me sort the dolls, *and* would you be willing to be here for moral support?" Janie asked hopefully. "You'll be paid for your time, of course."

"I would be glad to come over and help you, Janie. There were a few dolls left that needed some minor sewing repairs. When do you need me? I have a customer showing up for a fitting tomorrow morning, but there are no other appointments set up for the next few days. If my aunt is up to watching the shop for a while, I could drive out and meet you."

"Oh, wonderful! Would the day after tomorrow be convenient for you? Mr. Marshal is coming around one in the afternoon. If you could come over in the morning, there would be time to finish up and go through the collection. I'll make some sandwiches and tea for our lunch, and we could have a bite before they arrive. Does that sound all right to you?"

"I'll check with Aunt Bernie. Unless she has something scheduled, I will be there around ten in the morning. I'll only call if there is a problem. Okay?"

"Perfect. Thank you so much, Miss Monahan."

"Please, call me Mibs. I'll see you Thursday."

"Yes, thank you again, Miss...Mibs."

~~

Mibs joined the three ladies who had moved to the shelf of quilting quarters. Half an hour later, the satisfied shoppers headed to the door with several bags of materials and notions: threads, buttons, and zippers.

"Please come again soon." Mibs held the door as they exited.

Aunt Bernie joined her niece a few minutes later. "Now! You go take a break, young lady. You've been going all day. I'll watch the shop."

"Okay, Aunt Bernie. A little time off my feet does sound good."

There were only a few more customers that afternoon, giving Mibs time to unpack and place items on various racks throughout the shop. Extra materials, patterns, and accessories were stacked in the storage room to wait for future needs. As Mibs arranged the items in the store, Aunt Bernie updated the inventory report. By the time it was almost five o'clock, they were both ready to lock up the shop.

"Should I bother cooking tonight?" Mibs usually fixed something in her apartment, then brought it down to join her aunt for dinner. "Or do you just want me to run out and pick something up?"

"Picking something up or just having something delivered sounds good. After the busy day, I doubt you're feeling like fixing a meal," Aunt Bernie replied, just as the front door opened one more time.

A man's voice asked, "How about a different option? I could take you two lovely ladies out for dinner?"

"Jace!" Pleasantly surprised, Mibs smiled. Glancing at her aunt, who quickly nodded yes, she walked toward him. "I think we would both appreciate that option."

"Great! How about we drive over to the next town? I hear they have a good Chinese restaurant, which I haven't tried yet." Shutting the door, he started to move farther into the room when Mibs pulled him to a stop.

"Wait just a sec while I lock the door." Mibs let go of his hand and secured the lock. Then she led him over to the counter where Aunt Bernie was sitting. "You heard right about the restaurant. Their food is good, and they have a nice variety. My favorite is the beef and broccoli."

"I think they make the best egg drop soup," Aunt Bernie said. "And I haven't been there for quite some time."

"Then it's settled. Chinese it is." Jace slipped out of his lambs' wool-lined bomber jacket and hung it on the back of a chair. His dark blue jeans looked new, and so did his forest green turtleneck sweater. In contrast, the cowboy boots he wore appeared scuffed but comfortable.

~~

Before Jace entered the shop, he had sent the officer stationed across the street home, informing him that he would keep an eye on the ladies until the next shift came on duty at nine o'clock. The round-the-clock police coverage ended the following day, but Jace had asked the regular patrol cars to make frequent detours past Monahan's whenever they had the opportunity.

"Ladies, may I suggest that y'all put on some boots? It's already starting to snow, and I'm not sure how long it will continue to come down." He perched on the edge of a table and gazed out at the white flakes that were hitting the window, then quickly melting.

"Oh? I hadn't noticed." Mibs walked over to the display window and peered out. "Maybe we should stay in town if it's snowing."

"I don't think we need to worry. It isn't heavy, and we'll be driving on main roads," Jace assured her. Eyes lingering on her lithe frame as she turned from the window, he gave her a slow wink. "I promise I'll be careful about driving."

Bernie was already heading for her room. "It will be fine, Mibs. I'm going to freshen up if you want to count down the register." Turning, she addressed Jace. "We'll be ready in a jiffy."

Jace waited as Mibs counted down the register, letting her quietly putter around, setting the store to rights. The silence between the two of them felt natural, and neither of them moved to fill it. Mibs slipped upstairs for a few minutes. Jace double-checked the locks while he waited.

When the women were ready, Jace turned off the lights, except for the security lights in the front and back of the building. He carefully helped Aunt Bernie into the back seat before assisting Mibs into the front. After he climbed into the driver's seat, the hungry group headed out.

Chapter 25

The snow fell heavier than expected but light enough that the snowplows had the roads drivable by Thursday morning. Mibs parked in front of the Hornsby Estate and grabbed the sewing basket from the seat next to her. She stepped out of her car and took a deep breath of the cold, crisp air. By the time she reached the top of the steps, Jane de Bois was standing by the opened front door.

"Mibs, thank you so much for coming! I'll feel better having you here when the lawyer and the person from the museum come to inventory the doll collection." Janie clutched the sewing basket while Mibs hung her coat and hat on the antique stand by the door. "Do you need a drink or anything before we head upstairs?" Janie offered.

"No, thank you." Mibs shook her head and reclaimed the vintage woven basket that contained her threads, needles, and other sewing items.

Touching the top of the pale pink basket as she handed it back to Mibs, Janie admired the decoupage decal of an older style Singer sewing machine on the lid. "What a great basket! Have you had it for a long time?"

"Actually, it belonged to my aunt. She's had it since the 1950s. I've always admired it, so she gave it to me when we opened our new sewing shop."

When they reached the doll room, Janie pulled back and trembled. Putting her hand on the woman's arm and giving it a light squeeze, Mibs gently guided her forward. The housekeeper had placed a stack of boxes and several rolls of acid-free tissue along the wall.

Janie placed one of the boxes next to a group of porcelain dolls. Then, picking up a roll of tissue paper, she measured off enough to line the bottom of the box. "Jasmine and Jennifer always used special boxes and tissue when they sent a doll from their collection somewhere." Smiling, she added, "They would say that they were preparing one of 'our friends' for a trip."

"It's obvious that you miss them a lot," Mibs noted.

"I certainly do. Jennifer and Jasmine were part of my life for a lot of years." Exhaling a deep breath, she grabbed another box and cut off some more tissue. "I thought that I'd get these boxes lined while you do your sewing."

"I'll get started." Mibs set the sewing basket on the couch and picked up a bisque doll that she had previously placed on a corner ledge. It had been set aside, waiting for repairs on its beautiful, scalloped, French lace ruffles. Retrieving an antique, white-colored spool of thread, she turned on a table lamp and began working.

The two women worked until almost noon before they finished. Janie had lined all the boxes and cut extra sheets of acid-free tissue in preparation for packing the dolls to be sent to the museum. Mibs completed the last doll dress repair and set the small, antique Kestner doll carefully on a shelf.

"I wish I could have found that spool of blue thread that I left here. The color I just used worked well, but the other would have been the exact shade." Mibs suddenly remembered the small piece of blue thread that had been caught in the door's lock and realized that it was the color of the lost spool. A chill went down her back at the thought that her blue silk thread may have been used by Jasmine's murderer. She stood frozen with that thought until Janie made a comment. "What did you just say, Janie?"

"Blue thread?" Janie repeated. "I found a spool of blue thread a couple weeks ago when I was doing laundry."

"Where?" Mibs asked excitedly. "Where did you find it? Do you still have it?"

"Ah, let me think." Janie tapped her finger against her cheek. "I believe I sat the spool on the shelf above the washer. I'd forgotten all about it until you mentioned it just now. Do you want me to get it for you?"

"Yes," Mibs answered. "No! Wait. Let's get it, but first, do you have a small bag? Maybe a sandwich bag?"

"Sure. I can get a sandwich bag, but why?" Janie squinted, perplexed.

Mibs put her sewing tools back into her basket and then picked it up. "Even though both your and my fingerprints should be on the spool, I want to seal it in a bag in case the police want it for evidence."

"W-what? Why?"

"Come on." Mibs led her out of the room. "I'll explain on the way to the laundry area."

They had just reached the bottom of the stairs when the doorbell rang. Peeking out the window, Janie saw a man and a woman on the front porch.

"Oh, that must be Mr. Marshal and the museum representative. They're early!" Reaching for the doorknob, she shrugged toward Mibs. "And we haven't even had lunch."

"Ms. de Bois," Mr. Marshal said and gestured

toward a short, petite woman who preceded him into the entryway. "This is Gail Winston from the State Museum of Art."

"Hello, Ms. Winston. It's nice to meet you." Janie turned toward Mibs. "This is my friend, Mibs Monahan. She's been helping me with the doll collection."

As Janie directed them to the stairs, Mibs stepped aside. "Please excuse me for a moment. I need to make a phone call. I'll join you in a few minutes." When the voicemail came on, she left a message for Jace, giving a short explanation about the spool of blue thread. "Please call me. I should be here for at least another hour." Ending the call, she hurried up to the doll room to join the others.

It was almost one-thirty by the time Mr. Marshal and Ms. Winston left the Hornsby house. Many of the beautiful antique dolls were going to find a new home in the museum. The rest would be sold at an auction, which would be arranged by the law office. The money would be used for charity as described in the sisters' wills.

Janie pulled sandwiches out of the refrigerator and began to pour tall glasses of iced tea. While she did that, Mibs finished explaining the importance of the blue thread.

Slowly setting the pitcher of tea down, a shocked expression crossed Janie's face as she stared at Mibs. "If the killer used thread to slide the lock closed, and I found it in...." She stopped talking and headed for the laundry room just off the kitchen area. Mibs followed her and stood watching as the housekeeper moved her head back and forth between the spool of blue thread sitting on the shelf and a laundry basket on the floor. The basket was situated to catch clothing from a laundry chute.

"Since the sisters have been gone, the only laundry that comes from upstairs is from Mr. Hornsby. I remember now." Janie whispered, "I found the thread in the pocket of one of his khaki slacks." Horrified, she shook her head, staring at Mibs. "I also remember some small brown spots on the bottom of the right pant leg. I noticed them just before I put the slacks in the washing machine. I remember that I pre-treated them, hoping that the spots would come out completely." Putting her hands over her mouth, she moaned. "Now that I think about it, those stains could've been blood." Janie staggered.

Fearing that she might faint, Mibs put her arm around the woman's shoulders and guided her back to the kitchen. Settling her in a chair and handing her some tea, Mibs picked up the phone and redialed Jace's number.

After several rings, the voice mail clicked on. "Jace, it's Mibs. Pick up! Call me! It's important!"

Janie slowly sipped the sweet tea as she stared at the wall, her eyes wide with disbelief. Turning to face Mibs, she began to shake. "I can't believe that Mr. Hornsby would have anything to do with his wife's death. I've fixed his meals when he is in the house. I did the laundry and cleaning for him each day since the sisters have been gone. I'd know! Wouldn't I? I'd know if he were... if he could..." Her voice trailed off into a whisper.

Sitting down next to her, Mibs reassured her. "You wouldn't have known. And we still don't know for sure. But, Janie, you need to tell the police about the slacks and the spool of thread." She nudged the sandwiches closer. "Eat a little and try to think about something else for now. After you've eaten and relaxed a little, I'll drive you to the police station. You'll tell them what you found; tell them about the spool of blue thread and the stains on the slacks. Let them handle things. Okay?"

"No! That's not okay!" James Hornsby stood in the doorway, his face flushed with anger. "Neither of you are going anywhere!" He grimaced as he took a step toward Mibs. "Why couldn't you just mind your own business? I doubt if sweet, docile Jane de Bois would have given the thread or anything else a second thought if you hadn't brought it up."

Mibs stood, ready to run, but Hornsby lifted his arm and pointed it at her. He gripped a black, short-barreled pistol.

Chapter 26

"Stay seated!" James Hornsby demanded. He called over his shoulder, "Wendy, come in and keep these two covered while I get something to tie their hands."

A tall, attractive woman stepped into the room as Hornsby moved out of the doorway and headed toward the garage door.

"Miss Black?" Janie gasped, and her eyes widened when she noticed that the woman held a gun like the one Hornsby had pointed at them. "I don't understand!"

"Of course you don't," Wendy Black chuckled as she stepped to the side and leaned against the counter. "You never had a clue. Not even once in all those weeks when I came here as Jasmine Hornsby's physical therapist." She shook her head, fake pity in her eyes. "No, not you, but Jennifer did. She even hired a private detective to follow James." She shrugged. "Of course, I didn't realize that until the police brought me in for an interview. That's what they called it, an interview, but I could tell that it was more like an interrogation. The cops told me that they had pictures of James and me together." Moving away from the counter, she leaned toward the two seated women. "We had an affair. So what? Some people may think that's wrong. Well, too bad for those people."

James Hornsby returned with a roll of duct tape. "They can't put me in jail for falling for Wendy. As far as Jasmine's death and her sister's death too, there isn't any proof to show that I had anything to do with either one. At least, there wasn't!" He kissed Wendy's cheek. "Too bad the police figured out that I'm not the poor grieving husband that people think I am."

Mibs stared at him in horror. Hornsby directed his gaze at Mibs. "I bet it was you." He grabbed a kitchen towel and stepped toward Mibs. "It's too bad that you won't be around to share this information with the police."

"What do you mean by that?" Janie stammered.

"What I mean, my dear Ms. de Bois, is that the police will close the case when they find that you committed suicide. Then, I'll just wait until the estate is settled and take the inheritance from the will." He paused before adding, "*And* the millions that I embezzled over the last eight years and leave this little, drab town for someplace exciting." He cackled. "My wife's kindheartedness made it easy for me to persuade her to start a charity fund account and put me in charge." Hornsby sneered at Jane de Bois. "I'll let everyone know how sad I am that you took your own life."

"No! I would never do that!" she cried.

"Oh, but you would! I already have a note typed from that old computer in your room. It explains how you couldn't stand watching Jasmine, who was more like a sister than an employer, in so much pain. Then, when you found out that Jennifer was showing signs of the same illness, you knew that you had to take care of both of them, give them comfort, just like you have for years."

Mibs remained silent and watched Hornsby as he first wrapped the towel around her wrists, then rolled strips of duct tape around the cloth.

"Why the towel?" Mibs asked. "Is that so that

there won't be any ligature marks on my arms?"

"Very good! You do figure things out, don't you?" He grabbed another kitchen towel and secured Janie's hands.

Janie stared at James Hornsby. "Anyone that knows me would never believe it. I would never hurt Jasmine or Jennifer."

"Oh, I think they will. That's why I'm going with the mercy killing scenario. I think people will accept that better than a motive of greed."

"How will you explain *my* death?" Mibs' eyes followed him as he stood next to his accomplice. She could feel the bile trying to make its way up her throat but mentally told herself that she had to control the fear and horror she felt. She couldn't let them know how scared she was. "Or will I simply disappear?"

Raising his hand and waving it back and forth, Hornsby smirked. "Don't worry about the details. I'll figure them out as we go. I'm exceptionally good at adjusting to circumstances. Of course, coming home and hearing you two talking about going to the police with new evidence threw a curveball at our plans."

Hornsby seemed relatively calm as he retrieved a glass from the cabinet and poured himself some tea. Slowly finishing the drink as he pondered the situation, he rinsed the glass and put it back into the cabinet. Bending down, he opened the door under the sink. After rummaging around for a moment, he stood up with a package of disposable gloves. "Ah, here we go."

Hornsby snapped on a pair of gloves and handed a pair to Wendy. "Even though there is every reason that our fingerprints would be in this house, let's not take any chances. For example, it wouldn't do for my prints to be on the glass containing the poison that killed Miss.... hmm ...what is your name? Monahan? That's it, right?"

"So, we will use the poison on her?" Wendy questioned. "What about Janie?"

"I have an idea of how we take care of her," he answered.

"I have no intention of drinking anything that you give me." Mibs stared at the glass of tea.

He laughed. "I wouldn't expect you to. That's why I have another way of getting it into your system."

Wendy slid the bag off her shoulder and handed it to Hornsby.

Unzipping a side pocket, he took out a syringe. He displayed it in front of Janie and Mibs like it was a prize. Stepping back to the counter, he set the needle and the bag down. He reached into the pocket again and pulled out a small vial.

Wendy picked up Mibs' glass of tea from the table and brought it over to the sink. She dumped most of it out before setting it on the counter near her accomplice. He opened the vial and poured several drops into the tea. Then he swished it around in the glass before dumping the contents down the sink. "That should leave a trace of the poison for the police to find," he boasted. "It's the same poison that killed Jennifer and the same poison that's now hidden in the garage under your extra cleaning supplies. So, even more evidence against you, dear Janie!"

Wendy snorted. "We had planned on using it on you, Jane."

Opening the middle of her bag, Wendy removed a folded paper and handed it to Hornsby. "I think we should change the suicide note slightly to account for the poisoning of the seamstress." She nodded toward Mibs.

"Hmm... yes, just a couple sentences should be enough." Tossing the note on the counter next to the syringe, he indicated Janie. "But let's take care of Ms. de Bois first." He pointed at the frightened housekeeper. "I'll use your car and that well-sealed garage. It'll take several minutes for you to pass out from the carbon monoxide as it fills the vehicle."

"No! Don't!" Mibs started to stand up but stopped when Wendy stepped closer and placed the gun against her chest.

"Sit down," she growled.

Hornsby secured Janie's feet with duct tape around the bottom of her pants. "Sorry. I can't have you screaming or trying to run." He stuffed a dishrag in her mouth.

Turning to Wendy, he instructed her to keep an eye on Mibs. "I just need a few minutes to start the car and direct the fumes through the window. I have a hose that I can run from the exhaust. By the time we rewrite the suicide note and take care of this problem, Janie should be out cold. I can remove the tape, and it will seem like she took her own life."

Janie tried to kick and struggle, but Hornsby picked her up and carried her through the garage door.

The garage door clicked shut. Wendy pulled a chair away from the table, sat down, and stared at Mibs.

"How can you sit there while he kills an innocent woman?" Mibs asked.

Wendy shrugged. "I just won't think about it. I've decided to trust James to get us what we want."

"What *you* want?" Mibs kept her voice calm though she wanted to scream. "Killing people and stealing millions of dollars is what *you* want? How can you live with that?"

A flicker of doubt crossed the woman's face, but she quickly shook it away. "It's too late now! He already got rid of his wife and sister-in-law. We can't change that. We have to tie up loose ends."

"So that's what I am? A loose end?" Mibs glared, her voice rising. "Will you be the one to stick me with that needle and push the poison into my body? Will you watch while my life slips away?"

A red tinge ran up Wendy's neck as she glanced away.

As soon as Wendy turned away, Mibs jumped up, clumsily but determinedly grabbed the half-full pitcher of tea with the fingers of her bound hands, and smacked her captor's head. The chair slammed backward and hit the counter. The gun clattered to the floor as Wendy slid from the chair and landed in a heap. The chair teetered for a moment before it settled back on its legs.

Mibs watched the garage door momentarily before deciding that the best way to help Janie was to cut the tape from her hands and call 911. The motor of the car that Hornsby had started could be heard from the garage. Mibs hoped that the engine noise had covered the sound of the falling body. Then, maybe she could find a way to surprise Hornsby and get to Janie before it was too late. She looked down. Wendy was still out cold. Mibs was about to pull open cabinet drawers in search of a knife when she remembered the scissors in her sewing basket sitting at the end of the counter. Using her shoulder to steady the basket, she pushed the lid open with her bound wrists and reached inside.

A strong hand suddenly grasped her shoulder. Swallowing a cry, Mibs grabbed the sharp scissors, raising them as she turned to face her assailant. She nearly plunged the pointed weapon into the man who held her.

Chapter 27

"Mibs," he whispered. "It's me, Jace." He carefully removed the scissors from her shaking hands and pulled her toward him.

"Is Hornsby here?" Juan Mendoza had stepped into the room behind Sergeant Trueblood. Noticing the woman lying on the floor, he stepped over, picked up the fallen gun, and felt for her pulse. "She's alive."

Jace started to remove the tape from Mibs' wrists.

"Wait!" She gestured toward the side door. "Help, Janie. He has her in the garage! He's going to kill her with exhaust from the car!"

The two detectives immediately raced toward the door, each pulling out their 9mm pistols. Jace stood to the left as Juan, on the right, reached for the handle just as the door swung open.

"You call, Wendy?" Hornsby stepped in. "What's going...?" Seeing Trueblood, he turned, jumped down the step, and ran toward the outside door.

"Stop! Now!"

Hornsby pulled out his gun and tried to shoot his way out of the situation. He fired twice, missing both shots.

When Hornsby raised his weapon to fire again, Jace returned fire.

Detective Mendoza yanked open the car door and turned off the engine before opening the large bay door. Then, he lifted the semi-conscious housekeeper out of the vehicle and carried her outside to the fresh air.

Detective Trueblood bent over James Hornsby's body. Lifeless eyes stared as the blood drained from the two bullet wounds in the chest, right above the heart. Jace pulled out his phone and made calls to the police department and to the ambulance.

"Jace!" He heard Mibs call and hurried back to the kitchen, quickly but cautiously entering the room. He found Mibs standing over the now awake Wendy Black.

"I'll take it from here." The detective smiled at Mibs, who was holding a heavy glass pitcher menacingly over the half-prone woman. He secured the suspect with a pair of handcuffs before he took the pitcher from Mibs' hands.

"I see that you got the tape off," he stated as he examined her hands and wrists.

She nodded absentmindedly. "Is Janie all right? I thought that I heard shots! What happened? Is she okay?"

"Yes. Juan has her outside, and the ambulance is on the way. They can take her to the hospital to be checked out."

Mibs sighed with relief. "Oh, thank goodness." She staggered. "I think I better sit down. I feel like all my energy is suddenly gone."

Jace pulled a chair toward her. "That happens after an adrenaline rush. I've seen it many times. I've even experienced it myself."

"What about Mr. Hornsby? Did you capture him?"

Jace frowned. "He's dead."

The sirens became louder as the police and ambulance approached. "Don't worry about

Hornsby," Jace told her. "The EMTs are almost here. We should have you checked out after they take care of Ms. de Bois."

"No." Mibs sagged against his shoulder. "I'm not hurt. I was just frightened."

"Well, for someone frightened, you sure handled yourself well." Jace saw the syringe, note, and tea splattered against the counter and down the front of Wendy Black's clothing. Glancing down, he noticed a trickle of blood on the side of the suspect's face. "Better have the medics check you, too."

As uniformed police officers entered the house, Jace tipped up Mibs' chin to see if the color was returning to her face. "Do you think you can go over everything that happened after I give these men some instructions?"

"Yes, of course," Mibs answered. "But I want to check on Janie first."

Chapter 28

Detective Trueblood handed a cup of hot tea to Mibs, sitting quietly on the sofa in the living room of the Hornsby home. It was hard to believe that this was the same woman who fiercely defended herself and helped save another woman. He sat down next to her and tucked a strand of strawberry-blond hair behind her ear. Her eyes filled with angst.

"I was so glad that you got here before James Hornsby came back into the kitchen. If you hadn't shown up, I believe that I would have been forced to pick up the gun from the floor. I don't want to think about whether I would have pulled the trigger or not." Mibs' lips trembled.

Jace thought for a moment. "I believe that, considering the circumstances, you wouldn't have hesitated. If it meant saving yourself and Jane de Bois, you would've done what was necessary." Taking the cup from Mibs and holding both her hands in his, he lifted them to his lips and gave them a tender kiss.

~~

When Jace gently kissed her hands, it eased the cloud of anxiety and sadness from the day's events. Studying his caring expression, she sensed his strength and tenderness.

"You're a strong woman."

"Nevertheless, I hope I never face that kind of a situation again."

~~

Jace nodded. "Now, if you're feeling up to it, tell me what happened here. I can guess at a lot of it, but I want to hear your version."

Mibs started with Jane finding the spool of blue thread. She explained how they went into the kitchen after the lawyer and museum representative left. "By the way," Mibs said, stopping her recitation. "I tried to call you a couple times. Why didn't you answer?"

Jace sighed. "Sorry about that, darlin'. My phone was in the pocket of my jacket, which I'd left in my office. Juan and I were out checking leads on Hornsby, so it wasn't until I stepped back into my office that I realized you'd left a couple messages. I decided to drive out here instead of calling." Running his hand through his hair, he scolded her. "I wish y'all would've contacted the station when I didn't answer my cell phone."

"I had no idea that James Hornsby and that woman were going to show up. Then, we were trapped, and I couldn't call again." Mibs picked up the cup of tea and took a long sip before continuing. "So, you already suspected the husband?"

"Oh, yeah," he emphasized. "The problem was that anything we came up with was circumstantial. Even if we find Hornsby's fingerprint on the spool of thread, he could have claimed that he picked it up at some point before his wife's death. The fact that we found three stores that sold the type of candy that poisoned Jennifer Morris, and a clerk from one of them remembered Wendy Black's purchase, wouldn't be enough to convict them."

Jace crossed his arms and shrugged. "We had just decided to put some of our officers on eight-hour shifts to keep both Hornsby and Black under surveillance. If they hadn't attacked you and the housekeeper, they would still be out there trying to get away with murder." He stood and picked up Mibs' empty cup. "I'll get you a refill and add a cup for myself. Then, we can continue with your statement."

~~

Two hours later, Jace pulled up in front of Mibs' building. "Sorry, it took so long to get all the information and get things organized at the Hornsby estate."

"It doesn't matter now. Sadly, another life was ended, but I'm glad we know what really happened to Jasmine and Jennifer." Mibs glanced at the storefront window. Her aunt was leaning forward toward the large glass pane to see whose vehicle had stopped. "I better go in and reassure Aunt Bernie. She tries not to show it, but I know she worries about me."

"I worry about you too, Mibs," Jace said in a husky voice as he leaned toward her. Tipping her head up with his hand under her chin, he placed a soft kiss on her cheek. "I don't want anything to happen to you."

Smiling at his tender words, Mibs leaned back and peered into his eyes. "Jace, I know this day must've been as hard for you as it was for me. Thank you for coming to my rescue." She took his hands and held them tightly. "I'll say a prayer for you tonight before I go to sleep."

"I could use some prayers." Jace lifted their intertwined hands and held them against his heart before releasing them. He climbed out of his truck, walked around to the passenger side, and escorted

Mibs to her door. "I'll call you tomorrow."

Mibs smiled. "I'd like that." Slipping her purse over her arm and reaching for the door handle, she hesitated. "I know you have to get back and finish things at the station. I'm going to talk to Aunt Bernie, take a hot shower, maybe eat a little dinner, then get some rest."

~~

Jace watched until he saw her enter and close the door. He sighed, rubbing the back of his neck, weariness hanging heavy on his shoulders. In the line of duty, he'd killed a man in self-defense. Even though the man had been an armed suspect who was firing a deadly weapon at him, it still weighed on his mind. He'd turned in his gun, and would have to make an official statement to the internal investigations team. Since this was a small-town police force, he would likely be allowed to continue the case in a couple days.

~~

As soon as she was inside, Aunt Bernie engulfed Mibs in a tight hug. "Mibs, I'm glad your home! Are you sure you're all right?"

"It was terrible, but I'm going to be fine. I'd just rather not talk about it yet. I feel exhausted," Mibs explained. "Jace knew I was drained. That's why he drove me home. He said someone would drop my car off later."

Aunt Bernie moved her cane to her other hand and grabbed her niece's arm. "Come. Sit down. You don't have to talk unless you want to. I'll get you something to eat."

"Sounds good." Mibs docilely followed Aunt Bernie through the shop.

Chapter 29

Monahan's Sewing Shop remained closed for the remainder of the week. Bernice decided that her niece needed a break. The trauma of almost dying had left the usually vibrant young woman drained and disheartened. After some rest, ample comfort food, and quiet prayers, Mibs felt revitalized and recouped her agreeable and confident personality.

~~

Jace met Mibs at their favorite coffee shop, Blueberry Grove Café, early Saturday morning. He took it as a good sign when Mibs ordered a cranberry and orange muffin along with her coffee and smiled when he sat down next to her.

"You seem better today." Jace placed his hand on top of hers and gave it a light squeeze. He'd been calling or texting her every night, as much for his peace of mind as for hers. The detective hadn't been cleared for duty by internal affairs until this morning. He'd used the free time to get his kitchen done, even hiring a crew from the Home Improvement store to install the island and new appliances.

Mibs took a deep breath, let it out slowly, and nodded. "I do feel better. I even walked here this morning." Chewing on her lower lip, she contemplated the recent deaths. "Just the thought of that kind of greed and viciousness in the world made me sad." She stopped to take a small sip from her cup. "I had to remind myself of all the goodness in the world. I believe that most people are basically good. We can't let those who aren't affect how we live our lives."

Jace studied her quietly for a moment. "It's great that you can see things in that way. In fact—" Jace reached over and tapped Mibs lightly above her heart – "It's that wonderful attitude that you have in there that attracts me to you."

Mibs laughed. "So, that's what you find attractive?"

Jace grinned. "Well, that and the fact that you're kind of cute helps, too."

A blush spread across her face as she gazed into his eyes. "I think you are kind of *cute*, too, Detective Trueblood."

Two girls sitting at the table next to them glanced over when Jace gave a hearty belly laugh. "I don't think I've ever been called cute before."

Gathering the napkin and the wrapper from the muffin, he tossed them into the trash receptacle. He picked up his half-full coffee cup in one hand and held out the other to his girlfriend. *Girlfriend?* A few dinners together and sharing coffee at the diner didn't make her his girl. Maybe it was wishful thinking, but he would like to pursue the possibility. He also realized that he shouldn't rush and risk the chance of chasing her away.

"Are we going somewhere?" she asked, amusement and a flush lingering even as she took his hand.

Jace placed his cup down and held her coat up as she slid her arms in the sleeves. "Since we're both off today, I thought that I would take you over to my house and show you the work I've done so far. I have the kitchen completely remodeled, and I've started in the dining room."

Mibs readily agreed. "That sounds good to me. What about the windows you mentioned a while back?"

"I found a contractor who put in energy-efficient windows with trim and details that resemble the original style," Jace explained as they walked to his truck. "They won't be exact replicas, but it would've been difficult, less efficient, and expensive to restore the old ones. His crew will also repair and refinish the shutters and the decorative crown above the front door."

"What about that window on the roof, the one you described with a little roof over it?"

"You mean the dormer." Jace assisted her into his truck. He could feel her eyes on him as he strode to the driver's door. "I checked the dormer when I was going over the roof. It's in good shape. New shingles were put on it when the roof was redone. A little scraping and repainting should take care of the rest."

After they were in the truck and waiting for the engine to warm up a bit before driving off, Mibs mumbled, "Hmm."

"What's on your mind?" he asked, clasping her hand and holding it. His thumb traced gentle circles over her palm.

"Well, you did mention that we both have the day off." She paused. "I think that maybe I could help you with the remodeling in one of the rooms. Is there something that I would be able to do?"

He nodded, giving her a searching look. "It would be great to have an extra pair of hands. What do you know how to do? Besides sewing and fixing up expensive dolls?" Jace laughed at the wide-eyed gaze Mibs offered in response.

"Stop by the grocery store on the way over," she

directed as he pulled away from the curb, driving slowly through the downtown area.

"Ah, okay." Jace cut his eyes over to her in confusion. "Are you still hungry?"

Giggling, Mibs answered, "Not right now, but I figure we will be later. You said that the remodeling in the kitchen was finished, so I thought that I could make lunch for us."

~~

One of those big smiles that Mibs loved to see spread across his face as he said, "You gonna cook for me, sweetheart?"

"You asked what I could do other than sewing," she offered with an impish grin, happiness spreading through her. She liked being called sweetheart by Jace, his Tennessee accent curling around the word with far more intimacy than she had ever experienced before.

Jace grinned in amusement, shaking his head even as the two of them turned toward the grocery store. "I'll take it. But don't think this means you aren't gonna learn how to strip wallpaper."

Chapter 30

"I didn't realize you lived this close to my place," Mibs said as they pulled into a driveway just a few blocks away from the sewing shop. "I've driven down this street many times but never paid much attention to the houses." She eyed the two-story brick house, noting the symmetrical arrangement of the multiple-paned windows. Studying it for a few moments longer, she nodded. "I like the roofed porch and pillars around the entrance door. If I remember correctly from my art history class, that design, the triangle gable style, would be called a *pediment.*"

"Very good! I'm impressed." Jace gave her an approving nod. "You are full of knowledge. If you know about architecture styles, maybe you already know about remodeling old houses like this."

"Oh, no!" Mibs assured him. "I may remember some of the classic architecture styles that I read about, but I wouldn't know how to repair them." She turned to face him. "But I bet I could learn if someone was willing to teach me."

Beaming, Jace acknowledged, "I'm always glad to have eager help. I've got extra dust masks and gloves, and there are lots of things to do." He climbed out of the truck and made it to the other door in time to offer Mibs a hand. "Would you like to see the yard before we go in?"

"Yes, I would. I see you have several big trees on the lot," Mibs observed as she surveyed the yard.

"Some of these trees have been here for years.

Luckily, the property has a double lot, so there is plenty of room for them. The yard's been neglected and needs quite a bit of attention, but I'm going to try and get a majority of the work done on the house before I tackle the yard."

He explained that the property line was defined by hedges on the sides and a wooden fence along the back. The bushes needed to be trimmed, and the fence needed to be repaired and painted.

When they reached the backside of the house, Mibs noticed that the large patio had dead grass growing between the bricks. A rusty, charcoal grill resting in the corner was leaning over on a bent leg. Long, rectangular, cement flowerpots held nothing but traces of soil, old leaves, and a few volunteer tree starts. The peeling paint and sagging screens on the all-season porch seemed to cry out for attention. This property would take a lot of time and money to bring it back to the grand state it had once known.

"Let's go in this way." Jace motioned toward the steps. "It leads into the kitchen. You might as well see the updated kitchen before I subject you to the unfinished rooms." Slipping his arm through Mibs', he cautioned, "be careful on these steps. Some of the bricks are loose, and the railing is a bit wobbly."

At the top of the steps, the screen door screeched a loud greeting as Jace ushered Mibs into the back entrance. Shrugging, Jace joked, "I could oil those hinges, but for now, it's better than a security alarm." He paused. "I'm hoping that a year from now, this area will be a great place to sit and relax. The same company that replaced all my exterior windows is coming back next summer and redoing this porch. I want them to replace the glass with double-paned, tempered glass in double-hung windows. That way, it will be nice even in colder weather. I haven't decided on the type of screening yet."

Making a 360-degree turn, taking in the sunny room, Mibs nodded. "I can imagine how pleasant it will be when it's completed. Sitting in a swing or at a table and chairs with a good book in your hand could be very relaxing." Pointing toward the back of the lot visible through the windows, she added, "If someone cleaned up around that big oak, maybe put some shade-loving plants and flowers there, it could be really nice."

"Yep. With a bit of work, this backyard could be quite an inviting place." Placing his hand on her back, Jace pointed to the middle of the yard. "Look, there's a cardinal! I've seen a variety of birds back here. I should get a bird feeder for them." They watched the red-colored bird flitter around the leaves and finally alight on a sturdy branch. "We could spend all day watching nature, but I guess we should go in."

Pulling his keys out of his jacket pocket, Jace slipped a key into the lock. The new door opened smoothly. As soon as she stepped in, Mibs exclaimed, "Oh! Wow! What a wonderful mudroom."

Between the back porch and the kitchen, a long, narrow room made a welcome entrance. Mibs could smell the fresh wood and paint and noticed the walls, paneled in batten board. Hooks were attached below a line of cherry-colored cabinets. Against a wall on the right, water pipes and a drainpipe were visible.

"I'm planning on putting in a utility sink over there." Jace pointed to the pipes. "I've been debating about building a storage bench just inside the door. It would be good to have somewhere to take off shoes or boots after working in the yard." Jace ran his hands through his hair. "What do you think? Would that be a good idea?"

"Having a place to remove shoes would be a good idea." Mibs then added, "You could build something, but I have another idea."

Jace raised his brow in question. "What's your idea?"

"The last time Aunt Bernie and I stopped at Tony's Vintage Treasures and Fix-it Shop over by the community theater, I noticed a wooden bench. I think it was an old church pew, and it was nice and solid," she explained. "If I remember correctly, it would be the perfect size for this space. Then, you could put a boot tray under it to hold the shoes and boots."

He tilted his head. "I like that idea. I'll stop there as soon as I get an opportunity." Smiling, he questioned, "Or would you go with me if there's a time we're both free?"

Mibs agreed enthusiastically with that idea. Then, they proceeded into the kitchen.

Jace seemed proud of the remodeling job done in this room. Everything was new, from top to bottom. The green wallpaper with a rooster trim had been a bear to remove, even with the steamer he had purchased. Now, a muted, blue-green paint lightened the room. The new counter and cabinets, the marble-topped island, and the tiled floor brought life and warmth into the room. The stainless steel refrigerator-freezer unit and the gleaming oven and electric stovetop would gladden any aspiring cook.

After Mibs gave the beautiful kitchen a glowing review, Jace hesitantly pushed open the swinging door that led to the dining room. He stopped and studied the face smiling up at him. Slowly, he leaned down and gave her a soft kiss.

Mibs took a couple deep breaths before asking, "What was that for?"

Putting his hands on her shoulders, Jace gave her a crooked, half-smile. "I was afraid that once you see the rest of the house, you might bail on me. I figured I'd get at least one kiss in before that happened."

Chuckling, the girl replied, "It can't be that bad." She moved around him and marched past into the next room.

Drop cloths were spread across the floor—an assortment of tools sat in neat lines against the far wall. Bare, wooden beams were exposed above with new wiring attached, and chunks of old plasterboard were stripped from the walls, piled around the room. A layer of dust coated everything.

Jace stepped around a ladder to open a window, letting in a whiff of chilly air. "Don't say I didn't warn you."

Blushing, she paused. "Okay, where do you want me to start?"

~~

Taking her hesitation as a reluctance to get her hands into this mess, he replied, "Hey, you don't have to help. I shouldn't have asked." Scolding himself, he wondered how he could face criminals who would spout off vile and threatening names without it meaning a thing to him, but one glance from her, and he was ready to crumble.

"Oh, but I *want* to help!" she insisted.

Stepping closer and ruffling her hair, he lowered his head and studied her face. "You sure?"

Mibs smiled, gazing at him. "You promised to teach me to strip wallpaper. I'm ready for my first lesson."

His heart warmed and he nodded. "Okay, woman, get ready to work." Taking her hand, he led her down a short hall. "First, let me finish the tour of this place."

The hall led to a half-bath on one side and a laundry room on the other side. Backtracking to the dining room and out an arched doorway, they stopped at the first door. The door was covered with plastic sheeting.

"For now, I'm keeping this covered to keep out dust from the remodeling," Jace said as he moved the plastic and opened the door. He indicated that this was his temporary bedroom. It was the room his great-uncle had used for the last dozen years.

Mibs pointed to a slightly open window. "Isn't there any heat in this room?"

"I shut the heat vent in here during the day and open the window a crack, so it airs out while I'm gone. It'll warm up pretty quickly when I shut the window and let the heat in."

Closing the door, Jace led her down a hallway. The hall led to a marble-floored alcove facing the front door. On either side of the recess, an ornately carved staircase could be found. Twin stairs met in an open hallway on the next floor.

Chapter 31

Jace ran his hand over the curved railing. "This is nicked and dull, but it's solid cherry wood. It will be beautiful when it's sanded down and has a good quality clear coat on it."

They followed the stairs up to the second-floor landing. Three doors were facing the railing, and two more doors lined each end of the hall. There were three enormous bedrooms, each with a full bath and sitting area, one smaller bedroom, and a separate guest bath through the door at the end of the hallway.

"I'll show you the master bedroom. It's the one I plan on redecorating for myself. The other two along the hall are similar. The smaller bedroom on the other end doesn't have the bath nor sitting room." Jace guided Mibs to the first door facing the stairs.

~~

As she went through the old home, Mibs felt like she was going back in time, imagining the various people who walked these floors over the many years.

Without furniture, the room seemed enormous. An alcove was nestled in the far corner; sunshine poured into the area from a window. The second window brightened the rest of the bedroom. A bathroom was situated at the end of the room. The wainscot theme, similar to the library downstairs, was prominent in the bedroom. However, the wood was lighter than the type Jace had described as cherry. Ornate crown molding surrounded the ceiling. Carved rosettes connected the decoration to the trim around the doors and windows. The parquet floor was in good condition, the design intricate and eye-catching.

~~

He smiled as he watched Mibs survey the room. Her mouth was open, and her eyes glowed with amazement.

"Oh, my!" she stuttered, "th...this is impressive!"

"It's my favorite room in the whole house," Jace stated. "The other bedrooms up here are very nice, but this is the only one with the decorative floor and oak woodwork."

Running her hand down a wooden panel, Mibs asked, "Is this oak? It's lighter than the cherry wood you've pointed out in the mudroom and staircase." She indicated the trim accenting the room. "That trim in here is beautiful."

Joining her near the wall, he said, "Yep, that's oak, and so is the carved crown molding and trim around the room. I thought about staining it a darker color to match the rest of the house but decided against that."

"Definitely, don't change it. It's perfect the way it is." Mibs touched Jace's arm. "You won't have to do too much work in here, will you?"

Jace's eyes scanned the room. "Not nearly as much as some other parts of the house. I'll repaint the upper walls above the panels, repaint the ceiling, and clean and coat the wood. I think I can just do a light sanding over the floor before putting a new protective finish and polish on it. I have an electrician who has completed most of the wiring throughout the house. He's trying to keep as many of the vintage plug and light covers as he can." He pointed to the bathroom. "The bath needs a complete update. The fixtures probably haven't been changed in years."

Leading Mibs out of the room, he returned to the hallway. "If we're going to get any work done, we better get started." Hesitating, he added, "That is, if you're still game to learn a little rehab?"

"Oh, yes. I'm ready. What's the first assignment, boss?" she teased as they made their way back downstairs.

One side of a pocket door was open, giving a glimpse of a room lit by a large bay window. "Let me show you the den, first," Jace said, "or maybe the library is a better description." Sliding open the other side of the pocket doors, he guided Mibs around the expansive room. One wall was covered with floor-to-ceiling, solid wood bookshelves. The other walls were done in wainscoting; the lower panels appeared to be the same type of wood as the shelves. An embossed floral-patterned wallpaper above the panels was faded and peeling around the edges. In the middle of one wall was a stone fireplace, complete with a marble mantel. In the fourth wall, a bay window was highlighted by a built-in window bench. The parquet floor was scuffed and worn, but the geometric triangle and square design could still be seen.

"Oh! What a great room this must have been! I can imagine the shelves holding hundreds of books and the room filled with comfortable furniture."

"I'm anxious to update this room." Jace knelt and examined the worn design on the floor. "The floor needs to be sanded and stained, but I think it will be beautiful when it's done."

Standing up, he stepped behind Mibs and wrapped his arms around her shoulders. "Most of the work in this room will be cosmetic, so I decided to do the other rooms down here first. They need a lot more work. As you noticed, I had to demolish the dining room down to the bones."

They stood together in silence for a moment surveying the room before Jace cleared his throat and stepped away.

"Anyway, I thought since you're here to help, we could work in the living room today. How would you like to learn how to use a wallpaper steamer?" Jace led the way out of the library and across the hall to another large set of pocket doors.

When the doors were slid open, Mibs stepped into another large room. Wall-to-wall marble tile covered the floor. The flooring was scratched and had lost its sheen. "I bet this tile was gorgeous when it was first put down," she commented.

"I'm purdy sure it can be again." Jace paused. "I'm going to call my dad and get tips on how to restore and renew this marble floor. I've seen him bring life back into large areas of marble like this before." Pointing to the brand-new windows along the outside wall, he explained that they were ones that had just been installed. Then, he indicated the walls they would be working on.

Sad wallpaper with barely visible miniature rosebuds peeled off the walls.

"I'll be right back." Jace headed to a closed door on the other side of the room. When he opened the door, the stripped-down dining room was visible. Picking up a piece of equipment resembling a small tank with a hose attached, he brought it into the living room and set it down in front of Mibs.

"Do you think you can handle this?"

"Uh...probably." She examined the machine. "You said it was a steamer, so I imagine you fill this tank with heated water, and steam comes out the hose. Right?"

"That's basically right," he agreed. "Just think of the tank as a big kettle. This steamer is electric, so when it's turned on, it heats to a slow boil, releasing steam. The steam goes through the hose into this large plate. You run the plate along the wall, and it loosens the adhesive."

While the steamer was heating, Jace grabbed a hammer and removed a metal picture hanger from one wall. Then, he ran his hand across all the walls, finding and removing a few nails. By the time he was done with that, the water in the machine was hot. Jace held the steam plate with Mibs. Firm hands kept a grip on her hands as they ran it up and down the wall as far as she could reach. After several feet had been steamed, he showed her how to use a wide stripping knife to work the loosened paper from the wall. When Mibs had a handle on what to do, Jace let her take over the steamer while he worked on the loosened wallpaper.

After a couple hours, Mibs checked her phone to see the time. "I probably should wash my hands and put the chicken and potatoes in the oven, so they will be done by noon."

Jace nodded. "That sounds like a good idea. While you're doing that, I'm going to work on the top portion of the wall." Before she reached the door, he made a request. "Hey, sweetheart, would you mind getting me a drink? I think there's lemonade in the fridge."

"I think I can handle that." She winked and he chuckled as she left the room.

Jace and Mibs worked until the timer on the oven buzzer sounded. Mibs had made a salad to go with the Italian chicken and baked potatoes. It didn't take long to set the table and start eating.

Jace smiled when he finished his second helping of chicken. Patting his stomach, he announced, "That's the best homecooked meal I've had in quite a while. You," he pointed at Mibs, "weren't kidding about being able to cook."

Bowing, Mibs insisted that it had been fun cooking in this updated, sparkling kitchen. "Maybe we can work on that cinnamon roll recipe you mentioned someday." As she stood to collect the dishes, she groaned.

"Is everything okay?" Jace asked.

"I just realized that I've been using muscles I haven't used much lately. I think my shoulders are beginning to feel the effects of holding that steamer."

Deciding to call it a day on the remodeling, the duo cleaned up the kitchen, storing enough leftovers in the fridge for Jace to have another meal.

"Do you want to go to a movie or somewhere else?" Jace asked.

"Thank you, but no. I still have a few things to finish up at the shop. I plan on opening on time Monday. Also, I've already left Aunt Bernie alone a lot longer than usual. Even though the shop is closed, I should check up on her." Picking up her purse and coat from the mudroom where she had left them that morning, Mibs smiled. "Is there a gentleman around who would be willing to give me a ride home?"

Bowing, the amateur remodeler responded, "At your service, dear lady."

Peering back as they exited the front door, Mibs asked, "You're going to return and keep working after taking me home, aren't you?"

"Yep, I'll keep at it until I'm too tired or too hungry. There's a lot to do. Anyway, I rather like this kind of work. It relaxes me. Maybe because it runs in the family."

"Oh? Care to explain?"

"Maybe we'll discuss it some other time." Jace locked the door behind them.

A few minutes later, Jace pulled his truck into the parking area behind Monahans.

"You usually drop me off out front," Mibs noted. "You decided to pull back here for a change?"

Jace stared out of the front window without talking for ten seconds before he unbuckled and turned toward the lovely young woman sitting next to him. "I just wanted to talk for a few minutes."

"Okay. What did you want to talk about?"

He reached over and twirled a strand of her hair around his fingers. "You have beautiful hair and gorgeous eyes. You have determination and spirit. In fact, you have a lot of good qualities." Jace paused, searching for the right words.

"Thank you," Mibs said, pondering the unusual change in his demeanor. "Jace," she said his name quietly.

"Yes, Mibs?"

She chewed on her lower lip before placing her hand on his chest. "Are you trying to tell me that you would like us to get to know each other better?"

His mouth curved up in a half-smile. "Yeah. I wanted to ask if you would like to start officially dating—if I can consider you my girlfriend?" Moving his hand from her hair, he sat up straighter. "Would that be okay with you?"

~~

"Yes, I would like to get to know you better,"

Mibs slowly answered. "Just remember, that goes both ways. You already know a lot more about me than I know about you." She leaned forward and rested her head against his shoulder. Courtship, as her great-aunt would call dating, was a time to share ideas and beliefs, likes, and dislikes. She considered the fact that he had previously told her that he no longer attended church. Faith, belief in Jesus, her Savior, was a part of who she was. Perhaps they would discuss it later. Mibs sighed.

When he wrapped his arms around her, it felt so natural.

They sat in silence for a few minutes, lost in their own thoughts. "I better go inside and get a few things completed in the shop."

"Okay, and I guess I should get a little more done at the house." Jace reluctantly moved his arm off her shoulder.

Jace walked her to the door. He waited until Mibs turned the key in the lock, then turned back around. Touching his forehead to hers, he said, "I really like you, Miss Monahan."

"I like you, too, Detective Trueblood." She could feel herself blushing as he kissed her on the cheek then moved his lips to her mouth for a brief second.

Slowly stepping back, he reached around and pushed the door open. "Have a good afternoon, Mibs."

~~

Jace made sure he heard the door lock before he turned and headed back to his truck.

Chapter 32

Although Mibs had needed a little time off, she was ready to get back to her sewing. After she returned home Saturday afternoon and took a long, hot shower, the rest of the day was spent getting Monahan's Sewing Shop ready for business on Monday. With a bit of help from Aunt Bernie, she straightened the shop, finished a couple leftover mending jobs, and set up the supplies for next week's sewing classes. The two Monahan ladies had a late dinner before starting on a 500-piece puzzle.

As they worked on the puzzle together, Mibs told her aunt about her phone call with Whitney. Mibs had called the girl to see how she was recovering. She was doing well. In fact, Whitney's mother had taken her on a shopping spree the other day. It was while they were on this shopping trip that Whitney saw someone who caused her to take a second and third look.

"Mibs," Whitney had exclaimed on the phone. "You wouldn't believe how much the woman I saw on the Metrofield subway train resembled you. What do they call a lookalike?" Whitney insisted on emphasizing their resemblance. "She had a little shorter hair and was wearing an expensive designer pantsuit, which I would have loved to own. Well..." Whitney mumbled. "Maybe in a brighter color for me. Anyway, I'm tellin ya', it could have been *you* standing there!"

"That's interesting." Aunt Bernie focused on her

niece. "I was just thinking..." The older woman seemed to drift off in thought.

"Thinking what?" Mibs asked.

Aunt Bernie shrugged. "I've never brought it up before, but I wonder if you may have some relatives in the northern part of the state. We never knew who your biological father was, but your mother was in Metrofield when you were born."

"Oh! Don't even bring it up!" Mibs' head pounded. "If my mother had a mental breakdown and some guy..." She crossed her arms. "I would never want to meet him."

"I'm sorry, my dear. Sometimes I overthink," Aunt Bernie sighed. "Let's finish this puzzle."

They stayed up later than planned to finish the puzzle. Her aunt handed the last piece to Mibs. "You do the honors, dear."

"Why, thank you, Aunt Bernie." Mibs set in the piece to complete the picture of a field of country wildflowers before yawning and stretching. "I don't know about you, but I'm ready to get a good night's sleep."

"Oh, me too."

Half an hour later, Mibs fluffed up her pillow, pulled forward her comforter, and snuggled back with a book in her hand. Her phone beeped quietly, so she set the book aside.

Thanks for today, sweetheart.

Heart pounding, Mibs stared at the text from Jace. They'd spent the day in his living room, pulling down old, cracked wallpaper. The weary and worn rooms in the old building needed a lot of work, but she could almost picture them coming to life. The house could become a real home. She'd never felt such a pull toward a man before, which scared her a bit. Still, she was glad when he made it clear that he wanted to get to know her better.

I had fun.

I'm glad, my little wallpaper peeler.

Whitney said she saw my twin in Metrofield...

Twin? I thought you were an only child.

I am...I think...you know the story my aunt told?

Her phone rang in her hand, and when she answered, Mibs smiled at Jace's warm voice.

"Talk to me, Mibs," he offered, listening quietly as she shared her thoughts and emotions, especially those surrounding the idea that Aunt Bernie had unearthed. He said nothing for quite a while, letting her work through her feelings.

"If you don't want to know, Mibs, no one, least of all your aunt, is going to make you."

"I know, but..."

"How about this," he finally offered, "if you ever decide that you do want to find out if you have an unknown relative somewhere, then you let me know. You could submit your DNA to Ancestry.com. Also, I think you might have an 'in' with one of the detectives on the force. He could do some research."

"An in?" she asked, her body humming with happiness.

"Yeah," he laughed, "I hear he has a thing for you. Everyone has been talking about it."

"They have?" she questioned, falling quiet for a minute. "I'm sorry if that has made things difficult. I know you're new here."

Jace chuckled. "Mibs, I'm the Chief of Detectives on the force. Dating the sweetest woman in Havendale isn't going to make things difficult.

213

And even if it did," his voice lowered, "I'd still want to spend time with you."

"Oh," Mibs sighed, hugging the thought close to her heart.

"Get some sleep, Mibs. I'll talk to you tomorrow."

"Goodnight, Jace."

Snuggling deeper into the covers, Mibs smiled, opening her book. Although she thought that she would read for about an hour, Mibs found her eyes getting heavy, and the hardback copy of *To The Far Blue Mountains* slipped from her hands. Setting the book on her nightstand, she turned off the lamp and quickly fell asleep.

Chapter 33

A few hours later, the overhead fan swished softly as the bedside clock radio clicked over to two o'clock. Mibs' mind drifted into a semi-conscious state. Her tired eyes rebelled against the unexpected nudging from her brain to wake up. As her head cleared a little more, she wondered what had awakened her. During the first few weeks after she had moved into her apartment, loud engines from passing cars and other street noises in the middle of the night would cause her to wake up. However, she had gotten used to those noises, and they no longer fazed her. But something had disturbed her sleep. Lying in bed with eyelids closed but ears becoming more alert, Mibs listened to the silence of the night.

A slow creak, like an unoiled hinge, brought her eyes wide open. A second similar noise brought the realization that it wasn't a hinge. It was the same squeak that Mibs heard each time she climbed the steps from the shop to her apartment.

Someone was coming up the steps to her room!

If Aunt Bernie wanted to wake her, she would call on the phone or call out from the bottom of the stairs. With the condition of her hip, it was doubtful that her aunt could even maneuver up the steps. Mibs usually left her door slightly ajar to keep the apartment from getting stuffy, and in case Aunt Bernie called out for some reason.

When she heard the quiet swish as the door was pushed further open, she racked her brain for something nearby to use as a weapon. Suddenly, she felt a presence near her bed. Mibs reached over, hit the switch on her lamp, and grabbed the book from the nightstand. Standing next to the bed with a long-bladed knife in his hand, Nate Olsen glared down at her. The face that had once seemed attractive with its handsome features and dark hair now made her shiver. The twist of his mouth and the strange glare in his eyes made her wonder if there was something mentally unbalanced about this man.

"Get out! Get out of my home, Nate!" Mibs shouted.

Shaking his head, he said, "No, Mibs. I'm sorry to do it this way, but I must make you listen to me! Others have gotten between us and tried to convince you that we don't belong together." Taking a full breath and ending in a heavy sigh, the intruder gritted his teeth. "First, that college friend of yours, and now that *cop!*" Anger seethed with his words. "I followed you to his house. Why? Why, Mibs?"

Knowing that there would be no reasoning with him, Mibs threw the book as hard as she could, not aiming at *him* but at the knife in his hand. The hardback book connected with his hand and sent the knife flying across the room. Pushing the covers aside, she jumped out of bed and headed toward the door. Before she reached the exit, Olson grabbed her arm and pulled her back, slamming her into a tall dresser. Screaming and kicking, she tried to get out of his tight grip. Reaching up to his face, she ran her fingernails across his eye. He jerked back.

"You witch!" he yelled as he put his hand over his eye and bent forward.

Mibs made it through the doorway and started down the stairs before he caught her again. He grabbed her by the hair and yanked hard. She yelped in pain and slipped down onto the steps. He slapped her face hard, busting her lip open. Blood dripped from her lip and from her forehead where it had hit the dresser. With tear-filled eyes, Mibs glanced up to see Nate turn slightly and lean back as he raised his arm to strike a heavier blow.

Instead of coming down to land a blow on the fallen girl, the arm went backward as Olsen's body crashed down the stairs. Breaking and cracking sounds echoed through the building as the man tumbled down, busting balusters and splintering the handrail near the newel post. Gripping the rail, Mibs pulled herself up enough to see down the steps. Nate Olsen lay silent at the bottom. Mixed with the shattered railing, the end of a broken cane could be seen.

"Are you hurt badly, my dear?" Aunt Bernie's voice shakily asked.

From the moonlight filtering through the window, Mibs could see her aunt leaning against a sewing machine cabinet near the stairway. "Aunt Bernie, what stopped him? What made him fall?"

"I did the only thing I could think of," she said. "I grabbed the upper part of his legs with the crook of my cane and pulled as hard as I could." She gazed at the tangle of body and wood for a moment. "I guess it worked."

Sirens could be heard approaching, followed by screeching tires and running feet that stopped momentarily at the shop entrance. The door flew open, and a uniformed officer, with gun drawn, quickly stepped into the room and moved to the left of the doorway. A second officer hurried through and slipped to the right.

"Over here," Aunt Bernie instructed. "The light switch is by the door." Turning back to her niece, she told her, "I called 911 when I heard you scream, and I unlocked the front door."

Just then, Detective Trueblood rushed into the shop with messed hair, sweatpants, an unbuttoned coat over a flannel pajama shirt, and a gun in hand. As soon as he saw the officers had things well in hand, he made a beeline for Mibs, lowering his weapon.

~~

When Nate Olsen woke up in the hospital, he found that he had a massive headache from a concussion. He had a cast on his broken right arm. Handcuffs secured him to the bed, and a police officer stood guard at his door. Lieutenant Taylor was waiting to personally read him his rights and charge him with home invasion and aggravated assault.

Chapter 34

Monahan's didn't open as planned on Monday. Mibs wanted a day or two to let the swelling on her face go down and to have the stairs repaired. Thankfully, she hadn't been too badly hurt. As she sat at her favorite sewing machine putting pieces for an *Irish Chain* quilt together, Jace and a couple of his friends from the station fixed the stair rail. They had already repaired the storage room window the intruder had broken when sneaking into the building. The guys had been making quick work of the project and were tightening the newel post into place.

An enticing aroma filled the air. There was a large container of stew in the crockpot and homemade biscuits ready to go into the oven when the work was done. Aunt Bernie was resting in her room watching an old Doris Day movie, *The Man Who Knew Too Much.* The warmth and comfort in the building seemed to help everyone relax after yesterday's chaos.

~~

Despite this, Jace felt a momentary heaviness surround him as he watched the woman who had found a way into his heart. Even from across the room, he could see her swollen lip and bruised face. Jace hadn't been there when she needed him, just like he hadn't been there for Conner. The logic in his mind understood that he had only been a teenager and couldn't change what happened to his brother. His heart had never let go of the feeling that he should have been able to help him.

But now...now he was a trained police officer, trained to protect and serve. Why hadn't he protected Mibs? A couple days after her friend Whitney left, the extra security was pulled. Lieutenant Taylor had been told that the budget wouldn't allow the additional cost any longer. Jace felt as if he should have been more vigilant. He was thankful that Mibs was a fighter. If she had frozen in place with fear when threatened with that knife, hadn't screamed, and hadn't fought back, things could have ended much worse.

Pushing all those thoughts from his mind, Jace went over and placed a kiss on Mibs' forehead. "We're almost done."

"Great! I'll go preheat the oven for the biscuits." Mibs moved her chair back and stood up.

"Don't hurry too much. We still need to do a touch of paint, clean up and collect our tools," Jace replied.

Mibs leaned her head on his shoulder. "It's really nice of Juan, Brice, and you to do this for us."

"Hey, these guys would work all day if it meant getting a home-cooked meal," Jace assured her. "They're planning on leaving after lunch since they only took a half-day off." He gazed into her sparkling eyes. "But I'm hoping you won't mind if I stay here with you for the rest of the day."

"I like that idea," she whispered.

Jace smiled and nodded. He tilted his head and checked around the room. "Do I smell cinnamon or nutmeg? Did you make something besides the biscuits?"

"I didn't bake it, but we have apple pie for dessert," Mibs said. "Aunt Bernie called a friend of hers and asked her to stop at the bakery. She dropped off some pecan rolls for breakfast and an apple pie to go with the beef stew. Baked fresh this morning!"

"Yum! The guys will love that," Jace exclaimed. "Why don't I go turn the oven on for you? That way, you don't have to go up the stairs and maneuver around the mess as they're getting it tidied up."

Mibs nodded. "That would be good. You said that you know your way around a kitchen, so I'm assuming you know how to preheat the oven."

"I think I can handle that. What temperature do you want the biscuits baked at?" Jace asked as he headed back toward the upstairs apartment. "And for how long?"

"Four hundred and twenty-five degrees. The tray is in the refrigerator. Pull it out, please, and set it out while the oven is preheating. Then, they go in for twelve minutes," Mibs instructed. "I'll tell Aunt Bernie that we'll eat in about half an hour, and you tell Brice and Juan."

He gave her a thumbs-up as he kept walking.

~~

Leaning on her new cane, Bernice Monahan smiled as she surveyed the craft table being used for lunch. It was set for five people. The Blue Willow dishes that she had inherited from her mother were placed around the table; it was good to see them being used. In the center of the table, a beautiful bouquet of flowers brightened the scene. Sergeant Long and Detective Mendoza had driven over together, stopping on the way to pick up the flowers. They presented them to Bernice when they walked in, thanking her for inviting them to lunch. Bernice knew that they were the ones who should be praised for helping with the repairs, but she accepted the flowers graciously, allowing them to be gallant. Knowing that her great-niece had other caring people in her life besides her gave her peace. Stepping closer to the table, she straightened a knife by one plate, adjusted a cup by another. Memories from years gone by of her mother setting the table when they were expecting guests for dinner flooded her mind. The older she got, the more she thought about her mother and father and the life she and her brother, Henry, shared on a small farm. It had been a lot of work, but it had been a good childhood. Where had all the years gone? It seemed like time went by in a blink of an eye. Her musing was interrupted when Mibs set the crockpot on the shelf next to the table.

Opening the lid and using a large spoon to stir the mixture of roast, potatoes, carrots, onions, and thick, seasoned broth released a rich, tantalizing scent that permeated the air. "This is a big container of beef stew. I guess I did make too much," Mibs commented.

"Too much!" Bernice tittered. "You're planning on feeding three grown men. I just hope it's enough. I'm wondering if I should have ordered two pies."

"Oh? Okay," Mibs responded. "I'll go get the container of iced tea. As soon as the biscuits are done, we can eat."

"I'll get the pitcher of tea," Jace announced, coming around the end of a stand, which displayed quilting books. He was closely followed by Juan. "Is there anything else you need?"

Gesturing with her hands, Mibs asked, "What about the biscuits?"

"Brice is plating them now. He said that he'd be

sure and turn off the oven, too."

Juan grinned. "He's doing what with the biscuits?"

"Plating them," Jace chuckled. "Plating means moving them onto a plate to bring to the table."

"Well, why didn't you just say that?"

Bernice patted a chair at the corner of the table. "Don't worry, Juan. Not everyone does a lot of cooking. Come over and sit down. You gentlemen should be hungry by now."

Accepting the chair that she offered, Juan sat down and spread a napkin on his lap. "I definitely could eat." He sniffed. "The food smells delicious. I usually only get a home-cooked meal on Sundays when I visit my parents."

"Does your mother like to cook?" Bernice settled into the chair that Jace had pulled out for her.

"Yes, ma'am. *Madre* loves to cook. She makes the best *barbacoa*, slow simmering the beef with lime juice, chipotle, and cumin. I could eat it every day." Juan chuckled. "She still makes chicken *tamales* from her momma's recipe, wrapping the onion and garlic-flavored chicken *tamales* in corn husks and steaming them in the same pot she's used for years. And we always end the meal with *Tres Leches* Cake."

"Wow! That sounds fantastic," Mibs said. "Does she cook like that every week?"

Juan nodded. "It's her Sunday tradition. If I can't be there, she usually persuades my father to bring a serving or two by my apartment. But that's only if those who did show up hadn't eaten everything. I have a big family, so often, there aren't any leftovers. Unless I'm working or have another commitment, you can find me there for dinner."

Scooting his chair in, Jace joined in. "The rest of the week, Juan eats mostly take-out food. Isn't that right?"

"For the most part," he shrugged. "But I can scramble eggs and make chili and a few other things."

"Oh! Don't mention Juan's chili," Brice exclaimed as he approached the table with a platter piled high with golden brown biscuits. "I've had it before, and it was so spicy-hot that I could feel the heat down my throat and in my stomach for a week."

Smirking at his fellow detective, Juan shook his head. "If it was so bad, why did you come back for a second helping?"

"Well, I didn't say it wasn't good. I'm just saying that it was a four-alarm-fire-type of chili," Brice explained as he set the biscuits on the table.

"Brice," Bernice requested, "before you sit down, would you ladle out the stew? The crockpot is too heavy and rather hot to pass around."

"No problem," he responded.

Jace stood and picked up Bernice's plate, passing it to Brice. After it was filled, he placed it on the table. Then, he gave each guest's dish to Brice until everyone had a substantial serving of savory roast and vegetables.

After the plates were filled and the platter of biscuits had made its way around the table, Mibs folded her hands and asked if they would say a prayer. The prayer was said, and everyone started enjoying the food.

It wasn't until the pie was cut and enthusiastically devoured that Juan spoke up. "Oh, heck! I hate to say it, but we have to get to work." The young detective placed his napkin on his dish and stood up.

Detective Long agreed. "You're right. It's about that time. And I have to stop by home and change, too." Nodding to Bernice and then to Mibs, he thanked them for a terrific meal.

Mibs stood up and came around the table. She took Brice's hand and then Juan's. "Thank you both. It was so thoughtful of you to come over and repair those stairs."

Giving her a fatherly gaze, Detective Long said, "I'm glad it was the railing that broke, and not one of your bones." He squeezed her hand before picking up his tools.

"Try to get a little rest, Mibs," Juan suggested. "You've been through a lot lately."

He kissed Bernice on the cheek, thanking her for the meal. *"Gracias por la comida, Tía Bernie."*

Bernice answered in Spanish, *"De nada, Juan. Muchas gracias por visitar hoy."*

Juan grinned. "You speak Spanish well."

"Not as well as I used to." She waved as Juan grabbed his coat.

Bernice sat at the table, relaxing and sipping her iced tea. Mibs came back to the table with a storage container. She put the last of the stew in the containers and filled a small bag with the last two biscuits. Mibs had started stacking the dishes, utensils, and glasses when Jace returned from helping the other guys carry out their tools.

"Let me do that," Jace said. "You did the cooking. I get to do the clean-up."

"Okay, or we could do it together," she suggested.

"Sure, sweetheart. Whatever you want." Jace snapped his fingers. "Oh, yeah! I almost forgot." He walked to the chair where he had tossed his coat, then reached into the pocket and pulled out a long, narrow box. Bringing it over, he put it between Bernice and Mibs. The wooden box was approximately eight inches by four inches. The design on the outside had several white rectangles with black dots on them.

"Dominoes!" Mibs and her aunt declared at the same time.

"I found them in the back corner of a shelf in one of my upstairs bedrooms. One time, my folks brought my brother and me to visit Uncle Ezekiel and Aunt Gladys. We played dominoes that day. I haven't played them since and don't think I remember the rules."

Bernice slid the top of the container open and spilled out the contents. The one-by-two-inch tiles had darkened slightly over the years and had a soft, ivory color. "Mibs and I spent a lot of winter evenings playing dominoes at the kitchen table when she was younger." She moved the small tiles around, turning them up so the dots, which she called *pips*, were showing. "Dominoes, checkers, gin rummy, and puzzles – those were our games." Bernice smiled at her niece. "Weren't they, my dear?"

"Yes, they were. It was a good way to spend a snowy or rainy day."

"Hmm," Jace smiled. "Maybe we can clean the dishes, and then you can give me a refresher course on how to play dominoes."

"Sounds good to me." Mibs turned to her aunt. "Unless you're too tired, Aunt Bernie."

"Never too tired for a vigorous game of dominoes," Bernice chuckled.

~~

The dishes were carried upstairs. Mibs stopped

to admire the handiwork that had been done on the stair rail, being careful not to touch the still-wet paint. Then, Jace washed the dishes while Mibs dried and put them away. It wasn't long before they were back down the stairs and sitting at the table. Aunt Bernie had the dominoes in the middle of the table with the tiles turned over, so the number of 'pips' on each tile couldn't be seen. She had also put on a fresh pot of coffee and set a glass bowl filled with mixed chocolates on the table; cups, saucers, and napkins were positioned next to the candy.

"Hmm! I'd say you might be getting ready to win," Jace teased as he pulled out a chair and claimed his spot. "So, tell me how to play. I remember the term 'boneyard' but not much else."

The back door buzzer interrupted their conversation.

"Are you expecting anyone?" Jace asked.

Tapping her forehead, Mibs nodded. "I forgot that we had a delivery coming." She got up and headed for the back storage room.

"Wait!" Jace commanded. "Let me make sure who it is!"

Mibs flinched at his command.

"Sorry, Mibs, I didn't mean to yell at you." Jace gently directed her back to her chair. Looking at her still bruised face, he couldn't be anything but overprotective right now. "Just let me check, please." Back in defensive mode, he stepped over and lifted his coat, picked up his holster and gun, attached them to his belt, and slipped his jacket on.

The buzzer rang again just as he reached the back door. He checked out the window to see a man with a dog standing next to a delivery truck.

Chapter 35

Detective Trueblood unlocked and opened the door, opening it only enough to get a good view of the man he assumed was the delivery driver. He was about five feet nine inches in height, dark hair with a few white strands around the ears, a bushy mustache, and brown eyes. He was around fifty years old but appeared to be in good shape with a muscular build. "May I see your identification, please?" The comment came out as a command.

Scrutinizing Trueblood through narrowed eyes, the man slowly reached in his pocket, pulled out his wallet, and held out his driver's license.

The detective scanned the license carefully before opening the door further and taking a step out of the storeroom.

The delivery man stepped back and held his hand up. "Hold on! Now, it's your turn. Let me see *your* ID, please." The step back and tone in the man's voice triggered the powerful-looking dog standing by his side. The dog moved closer and growled.

Trueblood considered the dog before reaching into the inside pocket of his coat to retrieve his identification. As his jacket opened, the gun attached to his belt became visible.

The delivery driver noticed and smoothly moved into a defensive stance with feet planted, a slight bend to his knees, eyes watching every move. "Where are the Monahan ladies?" the driver asked in a no-nonsense voice. "And who are you?"

Lifting his ID, Jace flipped it open. "My name is

Jace Trueblood. I'm a detective on the Havendale Police Force."

The driver's defiant gaze turned into one of worry. "Are the Monahan ladies all right? Did something happen?"

Tilting his head toward the window nearest the back door, the detective answered, "There was a break-in Sunday morning before daylight."

The man nodded. "You still haven't told me if Bernice and Mibs are okay. I'd like to see them."

Jace said, "You seem more concerned than the average delivery person."

"The Monahan ladies aren't just customers," he responded. "I consider them friends."

Stepping aside, Jace motioned for him to enter.

"Thank you, Chief of Detectives, Jace Trueblood," the man said as he stepped into the storage room.

"Hmm," Jace mumbled as he realized that the driver had actually read his police department identification in the short time that it had been held in front of him.

To let him know that he also noticed details and information, Jace followed him in and commented, "You're welcome, William Andrew McBride."

Turning around, Willy gave him a slight smile and nodded. Just then, Mibs peeked her head around the corner of a storage shelf by the inside door.

"Is it okay to come out now?" she asked. "Hi, Willy."

Shadow barked and wagged her tail.

"Shadow, how are you, sweet lady? Would you like a cookie?"

The dog barked again, eagerly, and eyed her partner.

"Go ahead, girl. It's okay," he said.

Shadow took off in search of Bernice. Suddenly, Willy asked, "Miss Monahan, what happened to your face?"

~~

Mibs unconsciously put her hand to her face, covering her mouth. Jace stepped forward and put his arm around her. Motioning for Willy to come into the shop, he guided Mibs back through the doorway.

When Willy came out of the storage room, Bernice was feeding biscuits to his dog.

Mibs was seated, and Jace was pouring a cup of coffee. After walking up to the table, Willy picked up a mug and held it out. Jace placed his cup down and filled Willy's.

Willy placed his hand on the back of a chair and studied Mibs' face. "Is whoever did this in jail?" He turned to Jace. "If they aren't, I want to know all the details you have, and I'll track him down."

~~

Jace considered the person in front of him. "The assailant is heading to jail as soon as he gets out of the hospital. If you have time, why don't you sit down, and we'll talk."

Willy pulled out the chair, sat down, and took a sip of the hot coffee. He scanned her face. "Mibs, are you sure you're all right?"

"I am now. In a few days, you won't even be able to tell that anything happened," Mibs assured him as she once again brought her hand up to hide the swelling.

When Willy turned back to the detective, Jace explained. "One of Mibs' college classmates had become obsessed with her. He followed her here and began stalking her. He had already attacked her friend, whom he believed was coming between them." Jace went on to describe the break-in and attack. "It was Bernice and her wooden cane who stopped him and sent him tumbling down the stairs."

Shadow had moved around the table and sat down next to her owner.

Tipping his head toward the dog, Jace asked, "Is she a military dog or a law enforcement search dog?"

Reaching down and scratching Shadow behind the ears, Willy smiled at the dog. "Military. She was taught to patrol and search." Continuing to rub the dog's head, he addressed her, "You were good at your job, weren't you?" His face beamed.

"I noticed that she has a slight limp," Jace commented.

Willy nodded. "That's why she was retired. After Shadow was injured in a firefight overseas, they weren't sure if she would live. She survived but couldn't run and climb as well as required for her former job."

"I recall you mentioning you were in the Navy," Aunt Bernie said as she slid the bowl of chocolates toward him.

He smiled and checked out the candy; then, he took a good-sized handful before replying. "I'd rather not talk about myself."

"What area in the Navy?" Jace asked. "Were you on a ship or submarine, or in the Naval Airforce, maybe?"

Willy shrugged. "I was part of the SWCC."

Jace's eyebrows arched in admiration. "I've heard of them. If I remember right, that stands for Special Warfare Combat-Craft Crew. I also remember SBTs, the Special Boat Teams."

"Ah, no big deal," the former military man mumbled. "Now, Shadow here, she's a real hero. She even has a US Military Dog Medal."

"Really!" Mibs leaned over the table to see the dog, who had lifted her head. "I knew you were a special girl."

Regarding the dog, Willy nodded. "Shadow and I retired together. I think we make a great team; we're good for each other."

"Thank you for telling us about her," Aunt Bernie said. Indicating his coffee mug, she asked, "Would you like some more coffee, Willy?"

Chapter 36

Checking his watch, Willy shook his head. "No, thank you, Ms. Monahan. I still need to unload your order and head out. I have a short route today, or I wouldn't have been able to stay this long. I better get the stuff into your storeroom and move on to my next stop."

Willy made eye contact with Jace. "Why don't you come out, too, Detective Trueblood?"

"Sure." Jace rose, sensing that Willy wanted to have a word with him.

"Thank you for the coffee, Ms. Monahan," Willy addressed Aunt Bernie.

"My pleasure," she responded. "See you next time."

Mibs had the back door open and was walking toward the delivery truck when Shadow caught up to her.

Willy stopped in the storage room for a moment and gave Jace a signal to wait.

"It's pretty obvious that you care about Miss Monahan." Willy stood in front of him. "So, I figure you'll do your best to take care of her."

"That's affirmative," Jace assured him. "I just wish I would have done a better job of protecting her the other morning." He grimaced.

Willy's expression softening, the former Navy man said, "We can't always protect those we care about. I learned that when my wife died while I was overseas. No matter how well we're trained, how well-equipped we are, we can't protect everyone." Brooding eyes shone from the weather-

and life-worn face. "You don't have to forget, but you do have to file it away and move on. If you don't, it won't be long before you aren't any good to anyone."

Jace's shoulders relaxed, days of tension easing off. "Thanks, Willy."

Willy started to turn away but stopped and reached into his pocket. He pulled out an envelope. After hesitating, he held it out to Jace. "I've been trying to think of somewhere to put this in case something happens. I have the feeling you're someone who can be trusted."

Jace paused before taking the envelope. "What do you want me to do with this?"

The older man turned and headed for the door. "Just hold on to it until I contact you to get it back." Stopping, he added, "If I don't, do what you think you should do."

Jace slowly slipped the envelope into his coat pocket, then went outside. When he reached the back of the truck, Willy slid the door open and climbed inside. Mibs stood nearby, reviewing the inventory paperwork. Shadow sat contently on the ground next to the girl.

It took four trips back and forth with the dolly and several trips carrying smaller boxes by hand. Mibs had checked off the items and signed the delivery receipt.

Opening the driver's door, Willy signaled to Shadow. The well-trained dog jumped up into the cab and stuck her head out the open window on the other side. Mibs went up to the window to give her a goodbye pat.

Jace ambled over to where the truck driver stood, ready to get in. "I wrote my personal number on the back of this." The detective handed him a small card.

Willy examined the business card and then stuck it in the pocket of his jeans. "Take care, Jace Trueblood."

Jace watched as the delivery truck made a three-point turn before heading out of the parking lot.

Placing his arms around Mibs, Jace rested his chin on her head. "Do you have to put the items that were just delivered away right now?"

Mibs tilted her head back and gazed into his eyes. "No. It can wait." Leaning on his chest, she said, "I suddenly feel exhausted."

"Sweetheart, if you want to go up to your room and take a nap, I can leave," Jace offered.

"I don't think that I want to take a nap; maybe just rest my eyes for a few minutes." The girl took his hand and led him back into the building. "I think I may just curl up on the couch in the shop and put my head back for five or ten minutes. Maybe you can put your feet up for a bit, too." She stopped to set the lock on the back door and hang her work jacket on a hook. "Or, maybe you can read the directions on how to play dominoes," she teased him. "I noticed the instructions are on the inside of the lid."

"That sounds good to me," he chuckled.

"Oh, wait," Mibs stopped. "I wonder if Aunt Bernie is still waiting to play dominoes."

When they re-entered the shop, Bernice was no longer sitting at the table. "Why don't you go relax on the couch? I'll check on your aunt." Jace gave Mibs a playful shove toward the corner of the room before heading to the entranceway behind the counter.

Calling out, he heard Bernice's voice coming

from an area near the small kitchen. Walking just past the mini-fridge, he saw an open door. "Bernice?" he called again.

"Please come in, Jace," she responded.

Stepping up to the doorway, he stopped and smiled. The elderly lady was sitting in a comfortable, easy chair with her legs propped up. She held a book in her hand, obviously relaxing.

"You look comfortable." Jace folded his arms across his chest and leaned against the door frame.

~~

Bernice smiled back, taking stock of the tall, stalwart man. She could tell that he and her niece really cared for each other. Of course, it was still early in their relationship, but she hoped that they would be right for each other.

"I am comfortable now." Bernice set the book on her lap. "My hip was starting to ache, so I thought it would be best to take a couple aspirin and just sit back."

"Mibs is pretty tired, too," Jace commented. "We wanted to check with you, but dominoes can wait until later if that's okay with you."

"That's probably a good idea."

"Can I get anything for you, Bernie?"

Bernice shook her head. "I have water here. Don't think I need anything else."

~~

Kindness and care shone from the softly, wrinkled face. "Jace," she said, pausing for a moment. "I'm glad you and Mibs found each other. Be good to her."

He stood straight and stepped closer. Then he leaned over and placed his hand on top of hers. "I will do my best. I promise."

When Jace came back into the shop and made

his way over to the sofa, he could tell that Mibs was more than 'a little' tired. She was in a deep sleep, her chest rising in a smooth rhythm; she was softly snoring. He stood over her, smiled, and realized that she would be 'resting her eyes' for more than a few minutes. Scanning the room, he spotted an afghan quilt over the back of a chair. He picked it up and unfolded it, gently covering the sleeping beauty.

Detective Sergeant Jace Trueblood poured himself another cup of coffee, moved the bowl of chocolates nearer, quietly pulled out a chair, and sat down. Sliding the lid off the wooden box, he began reading the directions for playing dominoes.

About the Author

Joan L. Kelly currently lives in Virginia and enjoys spending time with her daughters, sons-in-law, and especially her grandkids.

A Thread of Evidence is the first in the *Mibs Monahan* Cozy Mystery Series.

Joan's philosophy is that life can often be difficult; fiction stories are excellent therapy. When life gets hard, escape for a while in a good book.

Previously published books, *My Big Feet, Hiding the Stranger,* and *The DNA Connection,* were written for younger readers.

Joan Kelly's YA work has been called "highly recommended for community library fiction collections" by *Midwest Book Review.*

Published by
Full Quiver Publishing
PO Box 244
Pakenham ON
K0A2X0
www.fullquiverpublishing.com

Made in the USA
Middletown, DE
11 June 2021

40748296R00144